Little Jack

IRIS COLE

©Copyright 2024 Iris Cole

All Rights Reserved

License Notes

This Book is licensed for personal enjoyment only. It may not be resold. No part of this work may be reproduced in any form or by any electronic or mechanical means including information storage and retrieval systems, without written permission from the author.

DISCLAIMER

This story is a work of fiction, any resemblance to people is purely coincidence. All places, names, events, businesses, etc. are used in a fictional manner. All characters are from the imagination of the author.

Would you like a free book?

[CLAIM](#)

[THE FOUNDLING BABY](#)

[HERE](#)

Table of Contents

Disclaimer 3

Part One *7*

   Chapter One 9

   Chapter Two 33

   Chapter Three 65

Part Two *83*

   Chapter Four 85

   Chapter Five 107

Part Three *121*

   Chapter Six 123

   Chapter Seven 137

   Chapter Eight 151

Part Four *169*

   Chapter Nine 171

   Chapter Ten 185

   Chapter Eleven 199

Part Five *221*

   Chapter Twelve 223

   Chapter Thirteen 237

Part Six *251*

- Chapter Fourteen 253
- Chapter Fifteen 275
- Chapter Sixteen 291

Part Seven 301

- Chapter Seventeen 303
- Chapter Eighteen 317
- Chapter Nineteen 333

Part Eight 347

- Epilogue – 349
  - Jack and Beryl 349
  - Mabel and Percy 355
  - Helen Nichols 359

Coming Soon 365

- The Lost Mother's Christmas Miracle 365

Join Iris Coles Newsletter 366

Part One

Chapter One

Jack Finch tilted back his head to gaze into the sheer blackness above him. His shoes were too small, and his toes had gone numb as his feet crunched on ashes and bits of half-burned coal. The grime above him was packed so close that he saw only a tiny dot of grey sunlight coming from the sky, somewhere far above, reminding him that a better world existed somewhere. A world that didn't smell of soot and unwashed bodies. One where his toes didn't ache with every step.

He closed his eyes for an instant as the memory washed through him. It had been so long that he hardly knew if it was a memory or a dream, but it felt real: arms around him, laughter in his ear, his belly full, his coat warm…

"What are you waiting for, boy?" an angry voice barked. "Get to work!"

Jack's eyes popped open. He bent to peer beneath the mantelpiece, which was hardly any higher than his head, at the stout man in dark clothes who stood in the centre of the room. Cloths draped the furniture to protect it from what would happen next.

"Go on," Smudge Blackwood barked. He shoved a brush into Jack's hands. "Get moving."

"Yes, Guv," said Jack demurely. Dread knotted in his stomach as he faced his task, but he knew he didn't have a choice.

The first part wasn't so bad. Jack held the brush by the long handle and pushed the end into the chimney, twisting and spinning it with practiced movements, his six-year-old hands barely capable of wrapping all the way around the heavy shaft. Soot showered upon him, gathering on the peak of his holey cap. He was lucky to have the cap; though he could feel soot trickling through the hole on its crown, at least it kept the worst of the soot out of his eyes. He blinked rapidly, trying to keep them clear as the air around him filled with the fine black dust. It stung his nose and tickled his throat. He cleared it hard, then coughed.

"Stop your fuss," Smudge barked. "Keep working."

"Yes, Guv," Jack croaked.

He felt a surge of relief as a small voice called from elsewhere in the house and Smudge stumped off to bully some other luckless victim.

Jack worked the brush up and down in the chimney until no more soot would come. He waved away the clouds of soot, sneezing, and then peered up again. The chink of daylight seemed no bigger. This chimney was filthy.

It would be a tight squeeze, but there was no putting it off.

Jack retrieved the stool Smudge always brought with them — well, one of the older sweeps would carry it, anyway — and placed it in the middle of the fireplace. Its legs crunched in the inches-deep soot as Jack climbed onto it. He pushed his brush up ahead of him until it stuck in the thick soot above. Then he rose on tiptoe, braced his back against one side of the chimney, and raised his right knee until he could brace it against the other. He shifted his knee against the wall until it felt steady. Finally, he lifted his left foot off the stool and braced his left knee against the chimney, too.

Thus squeezing himself into the chimney, Jack began to climb. He worked the brush into the soot and brought showers of it down onto himself. The air grew thick and dark; his cap could no longer save him. Soon it was too dark and dusty to see a thing.

His eyes streamed and burned, his lungs ached, and he coughed with every breath. Still he kept climbing, pushing the brush ahead of him, then climbing a few inches higher when there was clean wall to brace against.

"Jack!" Smudge barked from below. "Aren't you finished yet?"

His voice sounded a long way away. Jack's brush scraped a little higher, and he squinted up. The chink of daylight had widened. He could nearly smell the fresh air, nearly, but not quite. His lungs still ached with soot.

"Almost done, Guv," he called, then a coughing fit gripped him.

"Stop that fuss!" Smudge barked. "Get moving!"

Jack cleared his throat, struggling against the coughs, and moved another few inches higher with a painful effort of his knees and back. They both ached fiercely; his neck matched them, crushed as it was underneath the layers of soot as he fought to clear them. His shoulders felt crushed and cramped against the ever-narrowing chimney.

The brush stuck. Jack grunted with effort. He pulled hard on the shaft, but it wouldn't budge.

Summoning his strength, he pushed upward, and a heavy chunk of soot fell into his lap. He gasped with surprise and then spluttered in the dusty air.

"Come on, Jack!" a young voice called from above. "I'm already done."

Larry—one of the other sweeps. He'd give Jack a hand up when he reached the top. The thought encouraged him, and Jack braced his knee against another section of chimney and pushed himself up.

Disaster struck. The chunk of hard surface under Jack's knee, which he'd taken to be brick, broke away. It turned out to be a piece of hard soot that crumbled the moment he placed too much pressure on it. Jack's leg straightened and his full weight slammed down on his opposite hip. Agony shot through him, and without thinking, Jack straightened both legs and plummeted.

He screamed as he skidded down the chimney, knees and elbows skinning on the brick, soot tumbling upon him, the world dark and choking. He'd fall like a rock onto that stone hearth and split his head like a dropped egg. He'd—

Jack flailed, and his fall ended in a painful scrape. Relief washed over him as he realized that he hadn't fallen to the bottom; he'd stuck in the middle of the chimney.

Panic quickly followed it. Jack was stuck.

He tried to stir his arms and legs and let out a stifled cry. His left arm was painfully twisted behind him, the right trapped across his chest. Chunks of soot had trapped him almost upside down against the chimney walls. One leg folded awkwardly underneath him and kept him from falling further. The other was extended above him, pinned against the wall.

"N–no!" Jack cried as he helplessly squirmed. "Help! Help! Help me!"

"Jack!" Larry shouted. "What happened!"

Tears flowed over Jack's cheeks, and this time not from the choking air, but from panic. "I'm stuck!" he wailed. "I'm stuck!"

"Oh, no," Larry whimpered. "Not like Archie."

The panic in Jack's chest grew. Only a few weeks ago, Smudge and the children had struggled to free a trapped sweep, but when they pulled Archie from the chimney at last, his face was pale blue and his chest didn't move. Smudge had hastily taken him away.

"Help!" Jack screamed. "Help!"

Heavy footsteps sounded below him. "What in heaven's name is this ruckus?" Smudge cried. "I told you to do your work quickly and quietly. Now do it!"

"I'm stuck," Jack wailed. "Please help me. Please! I'm stuck like Archie! I'm stuck!"

Smudge's footsteps moved underneath Jack. He heard big boots crunching on the soot.

"Help," Jack sobbed.

"Stop that noise," Smudge barked. "You'll alarm the clients."

Jack held back his tears into tiny whimpers of sheer terror. His arm cramped agonizingly, the pain taking his breath away. The air felt too dense to breathe. His chest wouldn't open.

Grunts of effort came from below him, and a big hand closed around his wrist. Smudge gave an experimental tug, and pain lanced through Jack's shoulder.

"Ow! Ow! My arm!" he cried.

"Shut up, boy!" Smudge shook his arm roughly, sending more pain into his shoulder.

Jack bit his lip, fighting to hold back the screams bubbling through his chest. Then, Smudge yanked with all of his strength.

Agony tore through Jack's arm as the rough brickwork tore a chunk of skin from his shoulder. He screamed and fell, and a rough hand grabbed his leg. The next thing he knew, Jack tumbled into the light. He landed on the sheets draped over the carpet to keep it clean. After rolling to a halt on his back, Jack lay still, sucking in deep breaths of the wonderfully sweet air, his limbs twitching as he relished his freedom. His breaths quickly turned to sobs.

"Jack!" Larry distantly cried from above.

"Stop that," Smudge ordered. "You're all right. Don't carry on so." He grabbed Jack by the shoulders and hoisted him to his feet, then slapped some of the soot from his clothes. "See? You're all right."

Jack rolled his wrists and wriggled his toes, realizing with a shock that Smudge was mostly right. The horrid graze on his shoulder stung, but all of his limbs worked.

"Now finish the job," Smudge ordered, "and don't take long about it, either."

Dismay and terror plunged through Jack's gut, but he knew that to protest would achieve nothing except getting boxed on the ear. He hung his head, retrieved his bent brush from the hearth, and slowly climbed back into the chimney.

It was a quiet, subdued, and ragtag group that made their way home through the darkness that evening. The flickering gas streetlamps were spaced too far apart on the narrow street and offered only watery pools of insufficient light to punctuate their way. Jack had tripped on the missing cobblestones enough times that he knew where to avoid them, and he walked numbly along, brush over his shoulder, head hanging.

Buildings loomed around them, silent, lights shining in only a few of the small, square windows. They crowded close around the cobbled street, allowing barely enough room for a horse and carriage to pass—as if anyone who lived here could afford such luxuries.

The five children, Jack included, came to a quiet and obedient halt at the foot of one of the tall and quiet buildings. Smudge produced a bunch of keys from his pocket and unlocked the door, then stood back as the children filed into a dark hallway. They waited in silence as he locked the front door and opened the doors to the first two tenements on the right. Then the children filed obediently into the first one.

Larry rummaged on a shelf for matches and a candle, and the golden light was a welcome relief as it illuminated their tiny room.

Jack stepped forward, wanting to go inside, but Smudge's huge hand descended on his shoulder and held him back.

"You, boy," he snarled.

Slowly, Jack raised his head. Smudge leered down at him. His rheumy, always-red eyes glared from among deep folds in a soot-stained face. Smudge was missing half of his hair, and liver-coloured patches adorned his scalp, barely visible beneath his scruffy cap.

"You cost us time getting stuck in that chimney," he snarled. "It was your own carelessness that did that to you."

Dismay clotted in Jack's veins. "Yes, Guv," he whimpered.

"Hold out your hand," Smudge ordered.

He reached behind the door of his tenement—the nicer one, second from the front door—and withdrew a length of cane.

"Guvnor—" Jack began.

"Do as you're told," Smudge barked.

Tears stung Jack's eyes. He bit his lip and held up his left hand, then braced himself.

The cane whistled down over his palm: once, twice, three times. By the third time, it was almost numb, but Jack still felt the impact down into his injured shoulder.

"Now go to bed," Smudge ordered, "and no more trouble from you, boy."

"Yes, Guv," Jack whispered.

He stumbled into the children's tenement, and Smudge slammed and locked the door behind him. The other children watched with sympathetic eyes as Jack drifted to the pile of soot sacks at the back of the room where he slept, clutching his sore hand to his chest. Larry's mouth turned down at the corners, but he said nothing.

Instead, the older boy sat cross-legged on the ground and opened the small sack that Smudge had given him. As the other children gathered around him, Larry slowly extracted its contents and divided them up as well as he could. He finished with half an apple, a palm-sized piece of cheese, and two slices of dry bread for each child. It was the first thing they'd eaten since watery gruel for breakfast.

Despite his throbbing hand, Jack quickly sat up and took his share of the food. The apple was mealy, the bread stale, and the cheese smelled, but he barely tasted any of it as he hungrily gulped it down. They passed a tin cup of cold water around to wash down their dinner. Jack drained it twice to make his stomach feel fuller.

The water swelled it to the point where aching hunger turned into quiet discomfort. Larry blew out the candle—Smudge would shout at them if they needed more than one candle each fortnight—and darkness enfolded them.

Jack curled up on his side, nursing his bloodied shoulder and hugging his injured hand to his chest. The rough surface of the soot sacks chafed against his skin; their smell choked his nostrils. But at least he was lying down, his aching limbs finally finding respite. He closed his eyes—not that it made much difference in the darkness—and waited for sleep to come.

All day, he'd longed for this moment of rest to come. Now, though, he felt no relief; only pain from his hand and shoulder, stinging discomfort in his eyes and throat, and every fold and rumple of the sacks digging into his bony body.

He squeezed his eyes tighter shut and tried to think of something other than the moment of pure terror as he'd fallen through the chimney. Anything, anything…

Laughter. Warm, melodic laughter in an adult voice, something he so seldom heard these days.

His lips curved upward at the memory. He remembered bright eyes that wrinkled at the corners when she laughed, and gentle hands ruffling his hair, or gripping his hand as they walked across the street. Fingers brushing through his hair. A smiling face behind plates of hot food, as much as he wanted. He'd hardly known hunger in those days.

The word slipped between his lips as he hovered between reminiscing and sleeping. "Mama," he whispered.

There were times when he could barely remember her face, but even now, her voice threaded through his mind with breathtaking clarity. It sounded as though she was lying beside him the way she always did at night, an arm wrapped around his belly, her lips against his ear. "I love you, my little Jack-Jack," she'd always whisper to him right before he fell asleep. Sometimes he mumbled it back; sometimes he was too sleepy. He hoped that Mama had known it was true.

My little Jack-Jack. Warm tears washed over his cheeks as he slowly sank into sleep, the memory of his mother's voice ringing in his mind.

"Hurry up!" the angry voice barked from outside. "I don't have all day, you know!"

Jack bent and wrapped gripped two corners of the sack of soot. His hands already ached, and dawn had barely broken over London's rooftops, bringing a bone-deep chill with it. He shivered in his half-mended coat as one of the other boys, Mikey, grabbed the sack's other two corners.

"Ready? Now!" Mikey grunted.

Jack straightened, his shoulders and knees trembling with pain and effort. Together, they hoisted the sack through the door, half-carrying and half-dragging it.

Outside, the farmer stood beside his wagon with his arms folded. His sun-blighted face folded into a frown of deep disappointment.

"What's wrong with these children, boy?" he demanded of Larry, who staggered from the room with a sack of soot on his shoulders. "It's taking an age to load the wagon. I have two fields to seed today!"

"We're short-handed since Archie died," said Larry quietly.

The farmer scoffed. "Smudge needs to replace him, or I'll buy my soot elsewhere."

Mikey and Jack staggered to the wagon. Despite his thick calves and broad shoulders, the farmer didn't move an inch to help. His horse drooped in the shafts as though grateful to stand still for a moment. Its bony hips jutted as it rested one foot and let its head hang as low as the reins would allow.

Jack knew how it felt. Together, he and Mikey swung the sack, then hoisted it onto the wagon with a yell of effort. It landed with a heavy thud. The coarse thread holding its mouth faltered, and a trickle of soot fell out. Jack hastily squeezed the sack shut before the farmer would notice.

"That's all we have, sir," said Larry, dusting off his hands.

The farmer snorted. "Maybe I'll see you again next week. Maybe I won't." He added his weight to the creaking wagon and cracked his whip loudly. The horse spooked, shoes slipping on the cobbles, and then trotted off with its blinkered head held high in panic.

"All right, boys," said Larry. "Hurry and fetch your brushes. We need to be at the Westing house by daybreak."

"Where's Smudge?" Mikey asked.

"He'll be here in a minute. Look lively!" said Larry.

"What!" Smudge thundered. "Aren't you stupid children ready to go out yet?"

It wasn't his usual angry yell that caught Jack's attention. Instead, it was the tiny sound that came along with it: a diminutive sob, so quiet he barely heard.

He spun around. Smudge strode down the street toward them, his face twisted into its customary scowl. A tiny little girl stumbled along beside him. She wore a grubby dress that was far too big; she was permanently in danger of tripping over the hem. Smudge clutched one of her stick-thin arms in his grubby paw. Her red hair floated around her head in a grimy cloud. Tear stains streaked her pinched face, but nothing could make her eyes look anything but huge and bright.

"Come on!" Smudge barked, yanking her arm.

The little girl tripped over the hem of her dress and stumbled a few steps. She gasped when Smudge shook her, then burst into tears.

"Stop that!" Smudge ordered, shaking her again.

The little girl pressed her lips together in total silence. She looked so small and alone and afraid that Jack's heart felt like it was being crushed.

"We have a replacement for Archie," Smudge growled. "This is Beryl." He shoved her forward. "Give her a brush. Hurry!"

Jack jumped into action. He ran into the house, grabbed his brushes and Archie's, and carried them onto the sidewalk. Archie's brushes were covered in soot; no one had touched him since his death. But Jack didn't think about him as he held out the brushes. The only thing in his mind was the terror in the little girl's big blue eyes.

"Here," he said softly. "It's all right. Take them."

"Take them," Smudge growled.

Beryl yelped with fear and grabbed the brushes. Her tiny hands struggled to close around the shafts, so she hugged them to her chest instead. Fresh tears spilled over her cheeks.

"Come on," Smudge ordered. "We'll break her in at the Westing house."

He turned on his heel and marched away. Larry, Mikey and the other children scrambled to catch up to him, but Jack reached back and wrapped his small hand around the little girl's slender wrist.

"You can walk with me," he said kindly.

She started moving almost mechanically, her eyes glazed and unseeing. It was only after they'd followed Smudge and the others for several minutes that she spoke.

"Where's my mama?" she whispered.

Jack hesitated. "I don't know." He bit his lip. "Maybe we'll find her later." It was what Larry had told him when he'd asked the same question after being brought here.

"Where are we going?" she whimpered.

Jack squeezed her arm. "We're going to work."

"Work?" Beryl swallowed. "But I'm only five."

"It's children's work," said Jack, parroting what he'd heard Smudge say many times. "People don't fit in chimneys."

"Chimneys," Beryl croaked, her eyes widening. "We have to go in chimneys?"

"It'll be all right," said Jack.

He didn't know what else to say, and he also knew that those words weren't true. It hadn't been all right for Archie. It had nearly not been all right for Jack. But Beryl nodded slowly, and the tears stopped flowing, so Jack supposed it had been the right thing to say.

"My name is Beryl," she whispered.

"I know," said Jack. "Smudge said so." He paused. "I'm Jack."

She met his eyes. Hers were like pale jewels in her grubby face.

"Hello, Jack," she whispered. Then she gave a small smile, and her eyes shone all the brighter.

Jack's head broke through the cloud of soot and into the cold, clammy air. London's yellow-grey smog hung low over the housetops, but compared with the chimney, the air here was piercingly fresh. He tilted his head back and sucked in great gasps of it.

He'd made it to the top. It was always a relief, but now even more than usual.

He gripped the chimney's edge and scrambled out onto the rooftop, his feet stinging when he dropped onto the shingles. Mikey was already on the roof, scampering to the lowest edge, from which they could use a ladder to get back to the ground.

"Come on, Jack!" he called. "We have to finish this house by tonight!"

Jack stared across the vast rooftop in dismay. For a child who slept in a corner on sooty sacks, the thought that a single family could live in a home so large was incomprehensible. What did they need all these chimneys for? Why did they have to do it in one day?

Questioning it was pointless. If they didn't, they'd all pay for it with blows from Smudge's cane. He thought of Beryl, then ran across the roof as fast as he dared and shimmied down the ladder to the ground.

Jack followed Mikey through the servants' entrance and into the dust-sheet-covered house. Larry was in the kitchen hearth, working his brush up and down as soot cascaded onto the ground.

"Bedrooms next, boys," he called. "Smudge is up there already. You'd better hurry."

Jack's stomach knotted. He jogged up the stairs, praying that he'd been quick enough not to incur Smudge's wrath. As he reached the second floor, he heard it: steady, quiet sobbing coming from above.

"You stop that," Smudge hissed. "You stop that right now, or I'll beat it out of you!"

Jack redoubled his pace. Despite the ache in his knees from climbing up the inside of the last chimney, he took the steps two at a time.

"I'm warning you, stop it!" Smudge barked.

Jack reached the hallway leading to a row of large bedrooms. The doors all stood open, dust covers everywhere, and the sobbing came from the nearest one.

"Mama!" Beryl wailed. "I want my mama!"

Jack cautiously peered into the room, Mikey by his side. Smudge towered over Beryl's tiny form. Soot smeared her grimy dress as he shoved her into the hearth.

"Cry out for your mama all you like, little girl," he hissed. "She doesn't want you. Now get to work!"

"Mama loves me," Beryl wailed. She numbly took the brush that Smudge shoved into her hands. "I want her."

"Start working or else," Smudge snapped.

Beryl's hands tightened on the brush. "I won't!" she waited.

Smudge's eyes darkened. "Why, you little—"

"Mr. Smudge, Guvnor," said Jack, "where should I go next?"

Smudge whipped around, irate at his tirade being interrupted. "In the next room," he barked. "Where else, you stupid wretch?"

Jack ducked his head. "Yes, Guv."

"Jack, help," Beryl wailed.

Smudge shook her shoulder. "Push that brush into the chimney like I showed you."

"Smudge!" Larry called from below. "The housekeeper's asking for you."

Smudge's face twisted in fury. "Jack!" he barked. "Make sure she sweeps this chimney. If there hasn't been good progress when I get back, you'll both feel my cane!"

He spat the last words into Beryl's face, making her whimper, and then strode from the room. Beryl screwed her little fists into her eyes and began to cry.

"No! No, no, no," said Jack gently as he scrambled to her side. "It's all right. Please, don't cry. It'll only make it worse for you. Please don't."

Sniffling, Beryl lowered her hands. Her pale blue eyes shone between scarlet lids.

"Where's my mama?" she whispered.

Jack braced himself. Larry had repeated the thought that they might find his mother any day for so long that Jack had eventually stopped believing it. He decided then that he wouldn't say the same thing to Beryl.

It was Archie who'd finally given Jack the truth. Poor, dead Archie who'd helped him through his first few weeks sweeping chimneys.

"I don't know," he said. "I really don't. I don't know where my mama is either. Or any of them. I just know that the only way for us to have a good day is to sweep this chimney, Beryl. Then we'll get something to eat and go home earlier. Does that sound good?"

"Food?" Beryl whispered.

Jack nodded. "Not a lot," he admitted. "But there'll be food."

Beryl swallowed hard and gripped her brush with a courage born of pure necessity.

"Let me show you how," said Jack.

Beryl's face crumpled. "Thank you," she croaked. "Thank you. You're nice."

"I'll be here for you," said Jack. "Don't worry. I'm here to help you."

Beryl summoned a little smile. It made her eyes shine like beautiful gemstones, and made the world seem a little softer and warmer around the edges. It made Jack ready to do anything for her.

Chapter Two

Beryl sobbed quietly as the children walked down the street toward home, coughing and snivelling from the soot. Jack stayed close beside her as he tried to blink the burning irritation from his eyes. He'd cleaned an extra two chimneys that day and could feel the soot weighing heavily in his lungs.

"What's the matter, Beryl?" he whispered, drawing closer to her.

Smudge glared around, but when none of the children dared to slow their pace, he ignored their conversation.

"M-my hands," Beryl whimpered.

She slowly opened her fingers, and Jack winced. The new calluses that had formed over her palms in the past few weeks hadn't survived a brutal day sweeping chimneys in a huge factory. Red, bleeding sores covered Beryl's hands.

"We'll bathe them for you later," he promised. "Hush, now, or Smudge will be angry."

Beryl nodded and swallowed her tears. It was a skill she'd had no choice but to learn since becoming a chimney sweep. Jack wrapped an arm around her shoulders, which had grown bony and hunched like his, and they walked in huddled silence to the tenement building.

For once, no one had enraged Smudge that day. He marched into his tenement without looking back at the children. They silently filed into their own room, where Larry and one of the other bigger boys, Henry, set the heavy soot sacks down on the floor.

The children gathered in a circle in silence and waited for their dinner. It was slightly better than usual tonight: half a boiled turnip and a piece of fish each, still lukewarm and wrapped in newspaper. Jack wolfed his portion down, watching as Beryl slowly, slowly nibbled each bite as though to make it last longer.

Inevitably, it was soon all gone. Larry kindly gave Jack an extra cup of water for his sore eyes. Jack ignored the suggestion and instead bathed Beryl's hands with a strip of sackcloth he'd torn from one of the unusable sacks.

"Thank you, Jack," she mumbled as he wiped the soot and grime from the sore ulcers. Snores already rose from the older boys; they'd collapsed onto the sacks and immediately slept.

Jack smiled as he wrung dirty water from the rag, then bound it around Beryl's most painful hand.

"My mama also taught me to say please and thank you," he murmured.

Beryl's eyes suddenly filled with tears. She held them back as she ran her fingers over the makeshift bandage. "My mama always said that everyone should have good manners, no matter how small you are."

"My mama is very beautiful," said Jack. "She likes to sing. She works harder than anyone. Her friend Charlie always said that nobody in the world could keep up with Mama once she got to work."

Beryl smiled. "My mama is kind and has very soft hands." Her face crumpled. "I miss her."

"I know." Jack sighed. "I miss my mama, too."

"What happened to her?" Beryl whispered.

Jack shook his head. "I don't know. Mama, Polly, Charlie, and me all lived together. It was perfect.

Mama was going to marry Charlie; she had a ring and they always talked about a dress and flowers and things. Then Polly got sick. Mama spent all her time trying to make Polly better, but I don't think it worked.

I heard Charlie screaming and crying. I think Mama and Charlie were fighting. Then she came to get me and said we had to go."

"Did Polly die?" asked Beryl.

Jack shrugged. "I suppose. She must have, because Polly would never have let Mama and me go, no matter how angry Charlie was."

"Did your mama give you away, too?" Beryl asked.

Jack blinked. "Your mama gave you away?"

"I think so. One day we went for a walk and she said to wait by a tree. So I did. And then a man came and said that Mama said to go with him. So I did. And I never saw Mama again," said Beryl. "The man hid me away for a few days and then Smudge bought me from him."

"I'm sorry," Jack murmured.

"What about you?" Beryl asked. "Where's your mama?"

Jack lay down on the soot sacks, hands interlaced behind his head, and stared up at the grimy ceiling. The thin boards served as the floor for the story above; they could see people's feet moving around through the cracks.

"Still in the workhouse, I suppose," said Jack. "She would never have given me away, never. I thought she had, for a little while, until I understood what the workhouse was."

"Mama says workhouses are horrid," said Beryl.

Jack nodded. "That's true. They took me away from her when we got there. I cried and cried for her, and she said she was sorry, but first I thought she'd thrown me away. But later I used to see her looking through the window when we came inside, and I knew she still loved me. I knew she'd come to find me, someday…" His voice trailed off.

"But you got out of the workhouse," said Beryl. "And she's still there."

"I think so," said Jack. "I don't know. Smudge got me from the workhouse. I didn't want to go. I wanted to stay with Mama. But I didn't really have a choice. I know this, though, Beryl." Jack gazed at her as she curled up on the sacks beside him. "When Mama gets out of the workhouse, she'll come for me."

"You think so?" said Beryl.

"I know so," said Jack. "She'll never leave me. She'll search for me until she finds me, I know she will."

"But what then?" Beryl asked. "She didn't marry Charlie, so what will she do?"

"I don't know, but she'll work it out." Jack closed his eyes and smiled. "When I was little, she used to tell me stories about a beautiful farm in the country. There were pigs, cows, and horses there, and big green fields. She said that maybe someday we'd go back to the farm and she'd show me what it was like. Maybe, when she finds us, we'll all go back to the farm together."

"I like that," Beryl murmured. "I'd like to see a farm one day."

"She'll find us," Jack whispered. "I know she will."

The thought filled him with steady warmth despite the chill that always whistled through the floorboards, and it gently lulled Jack to sleep.

Mabel Mitchell smiled as she watched the big chestnut horse toiling up the hill toward the farmhouse.

The sturdy young mare, whom she'd named Polly after a late friend, was shining like a copper penny in the sun. Her farm hand, Bobby, strode along behind her, whistling cheerfully above the jingle of harness as the big animal plodded into the stable yard.

"Afternoon, Bobby!" Mabel called. "How did it go?"

"Afternoon, Mrs. Mitchell." Bobby doffed his cap. "It was real good. We've mowed the whole south field now. We'll get that last cutting put up well before the frost."

"Excellent." Mabel smiled. "We'll need it for the sheep."

Her new flock grazed in the meadow beneath the branches of a spreading old oak tree. They were fat and prosperous, their coats growing shaggy with wool; she hoped that they would pay back their investment at shearing time in the spring.

No, not hoped. Mabel raised her eyes to heaven and smiled. She could do better than hope. She could pray.

A pang ran through her. *Lord,* she prayed silently, *be with my Jack-Jack.*

It was a prayer that she quietly offered a dozen times a day.

Sadness and longing swept through her like a cold wind.

Wrapping her arms around her growing belly, Mabel strode across the farmyard to the large barn as Bobby led Polly into her stall. Quietly, she unbuckled Polly's bridle and pulled it off the big animal's sweaty head, then caressed the long nose with gentle hands.

"Easy there, Mrs. Mitchell," said Bobby, hauling the harness off Polly's back. "Shouldn't you go inside and put your feet up?"

Mabel smiled. "I'm quite all right, Bobby."

"I'm just saying." Bobby delicately cleared his throat. "You know... in your condition."

Mabel chuckled. "I'm not ill." She ran a hand over her belly. "When I was expecting Jack, I ran this farm single-handedly."

Bobby rubbed the back of his neck, desperately uncomfortable. "Yes, ma'am. But all I'm saying is that you don't have to do that no more."

Mabel blinked. She cupped her hands underneath her belly, thinking of the way she'd staggered through her abusive late husband's fields as Jack grew inside her. Bobby was right. She had no need to that anymore. These were her fields now, and they prospered under her loving attention.

"Mae!" a gentle voice called from the house. "Where are you, my love?"

"Coming!" Mabel called.

She smiled at Bobby, fed Polly an apple from the freshly harvested barrel, and hurried across the farmyard to the spacious kitchen. Their maidservant was chopping carrots for dinner; Mabel paused to smile at her before moving into the living room.

A fire roared in the hearth, but it could not match the warmth of her dear husband's smile as he stepped through the front door.

"Hello, darling." Percy beamed.

Mabel wrapped her arms around him. He planted a gentle kiss on her head as she hugged him.

"Mmm, I missed you," she said.

"I only left this morning." Percy chuckled.

"I still missed you," said Mabel. "How about some tea?"

"I'll bring you a tray, Mrs. Mitchell," the girl called from the kitchen. "No carrying things!"

"You'd swear I had a broken back," Mabel grumbled.

"We're all excited for the little one, that's all." Percy grinned. "Sit with me."

He led her to the sofa by the fire, and they sat down side by side, gazing at the crackling flames as dusk settled over the farm's gentle hills outside.

"How was business today?" Mabel asked.

"Good." Percy nodded. "I believe Farmer Thornton's case will go to court. Hopefully we can get the man who robbed him convicted."

"With you representing him, I'm sure you will," said Mabel.

Percy smiled and hugged her. "Thank you, darling."

"Our village is lucky to have a lawyer like you," said Mabel. "I know I am."

Percy squeezed her shoulders. "I'm grateful you think so, my love. There are times when I wish—"

"Oh!" Mabel cried.

"What? What?" Percy straightened. "Are you all right? Are you in pain?"

"No!" Mabel laughed as a smile stretched over her face. "It's the baby. It's moving."

Percy's eyes widened. Mabel pressed her hand to her belly, then grabbed his free hand and held it to the same spot.

She saw utter wonder blossom over his gentle face as he felt their child stirring beneath her skin. His soft eyes sparkled. A childlike giggle of pure glee rose from his lips.

"Oh, Mae," he whispered. "Our baby is really alive in there."

"Yes, it is." Mabel smiled into his eyes. "I can't wait to raise this little one with you."

"Neither can I." Percy gently pressed his lips to her forehead. "I love you."

The simple perfection of the moment soaked into her skin. It was so different from her last pregnancy, spent in terror and pain, labouring under Ned's abuse, then working at a rag factory. She'd had Jack in an alley; she would have died and lost him if Polly hadn't come to save her.

But now, she was cherished, protected, loved. Everything in her life was a thousand times better... but perhaps not in Jack's.

Tears stung her eyes. The pregnancy made them spill over all the more easily, and before she knew it, she had her head in her hands and was sobbing her heart out.

"Mae!" said Percy in dismay. "What's the matter?"

"I'm sorry," Mabel sobbed. "I'm so sorry."

"Oh, my darling." Percy wrapped her in his arms, understanding, and pressed her face close to his chest. "I know. I know. I wish Jack was here, too."

The sound of his name only made her cry harder. Percy cradled her, not protesting, never complaining that Jack's absence ruined so many of their life's beautiful moments even though it wasn't his fault that Mabel had lost him in that dreadful workhouse.

Her tears slowly subsided. The maidservant brought them tea and biscuits, and Mabel took a few sips to soothe herself.

"We'll find him, Mae." Percy hooked a strand of her hair behind her ear. "I have court in London again in a few weeks. I'll visit the new investigator."

"Are you sure of this one, darling?" Mabel asked.

Percy sighed. "I truly am. He has excellent references, which the previous one didn't. I'm sorry I ever hired him. All he did was to take our money in the eighteen months we paid him to look for Jack... I doubt he ever lifted a finger."

"Eighteen months," said Mabel. Pain pierced her at the thought of the suffering her poor child could have endured on London's streets in that time.

"It's different now," Percy murmured. "Mr. Martins is sending me regular letters. He might not have found anything yet, but he's working hard and doing all the right things. I know he'll find something for us soon, my darling."

"I believe you." Mabel dried her eyes. "Thank you Percy, my love."

"Of course." Percy kissed her cheek. "I'll never stop searching for him. He's your child, and I married you. That makes him my child, too."

Mabel leaned against him, gratitude washing through her. "The Lord is faithful," she murmured. "He can do anything. I trust Him."

"Amen," said Percy.

Beryl's grunts of effort rose echoed through the wall. Jack winced with each one, hearing the edge of fear and frustration in them. He was finishing up with a chimney, which he'd already swept to the top, by shovelling soot into a sack from the hearth. This was one of the fanciest houses he'd seen; every bedroom had its own fireplace.

"Come on, child!" Smudge barked. "We don't have all day!"

Jack hastily shovelled a last scoop of soot into the sack and then tied the mouth with a piece of rough skin that moved painfully over his dry, chapped hands. He glanced around, making sure the hearth was perfectly clean. If it wasn't, Smudge and his cane would punish him for it.

"What are you waiting for?" Smudge demanded. "Get to work!"

Beryl's next grunt came coupled with a sob. Anger and sorrow washed through Jack, and he turned on his heel and strode from the room.

When he walked into the adjoining bedroom, Smudge bent forward, peering into the chimney. Judging from Beryl's cries of effort, she hadn't gotten much more than six or seven feet off the ground.

"What are you doing in there?" Smudge yelled.

"I'm all done, Guv," said Jack. "I'll do this one, too."

Smudge whirled around, eyes narrowed. Beryl went suddenly very quiet.

"What are you talking about?" Smudge snapped.

"I've finished my last chimney for the day. Let me do this one," Jack wheedled. "I can finish it faster than she can, Guv. Then we'll be done in record time."

Smudge sneered. "What do you care?"

"The house owner will be happy, Guv," said Jack.

It was always the right button to push with Smudge.

"I don't believe you," the sweep snarled. "You can't be finished."

He strode to the hallway and put his head around the door, then gave a begrudging grunt when he saw the filled soot sack and the spotless hearth.

"Very well," Smudge snapped. "But make it quick!"

He stalked out of the room as Beryl shimmied down and landed heavily on her feet in the fireplace.

"Thank you," she whispered. Tears of fear and frustration had washed clean trails over the soot on her cheeks.

Jack smiled at her, then climbed on her stool and started to shimmy up the chimney. She passed him a brush from below, and he wedged it against the heavy soot. It was so thick that he could see no daylight from above.

"It's really hard and stuck," he muttered, hitting it again with the brush. "I can see why you couldn't budge it."

"Oh, Jack, you have to hurry," Beryl cried. "Smudge will be back any minute, you know he will."

Jack was all too aware. Small blisters on his hands still burned from the last caning he'd received for not cleaning a chimney quickly enough. He could only hope, if he got this done fast, that Beryl would escape a similar fate.

He gritted his teeth and slammed the brush repeatedly into the thick soot. A few flakes tumbled down, but most of the soot remained.

"Turn the brush over for me." Jack passed it down to Beryl.

She handed it back, handle first, and Jack slammed the hard wood against the soot. Finally, a few chunks broke loose and broke on the hearth floor with heavy puffs.

"It's working!" Beryl hissed. "Hurry! He's coming!"

Jack moved as quickly as he could. He pounded the brush into the soot over and over again, breaking off bits the size of his fist, but progress remained painfully slow. Minutes slid by; Jack climbed inches, then a few feet, and the thick soot left rinds that dug into his back and knees.

His arms trembled with pain and effort as he rammed the soot with his brush handle as hard as he could.

Smudge's footsteps resounded in the room. Jack redoubled his efforts.

"What are you doing?" Smudge bellowed. "You're not even halfway up yet!"

"Yes, Guv." Jack spluttered against the soot that clogged his eyes and nostrils. "It's hard-packed in here, Guv."

"We don't have time for this," Smudge snapped. "Get moving, you lazy little wretch!"

"Yes, Guv." Jack couldn't go any faster; his trembling hands barely allowed him to hold the brush at all. His fingers were numbly sore from the pounding. He wrapped them more tightly around the handle and scraped a chunk of soot from the brickwork in front of him. It hit the ground with a thump and broke apart.

Maybe seeing the thick-packed soot would show Smudge that Jack was serious. Maybe, for once, he would be reasonable.

It was a foolish and crazy hope.

"I'm warning you, boy," Smudge roared a few minutes later, "if you don't start making better progress, you'll be sorry!"

"He's doing his best," Beryl piped up suddenly.

There was a terrible, ringing slap—the sound of flesh on flesh.

"Shut up!" Smudge snarled.

Tears stung Jack's eyes, and not only from the thick, choking soot. Rage gave him a burst of strength.

He worked another piece of soot free and kept going, but it wasn't enough for Smudge.

"What are you doing?" Beryl cried.

"Go outside with the other children. Now!" Smudge bellowed.

Beryl's running feet faded into the distance. Jack was alone, and Smudge scraped around in the hearth beneath. Terror and dismay filled him. He'd heard stories from Larry and Archie about the things Smudge could do if one was too slow.

"It's really hard, Guv," Jack called. "I'm getting there. A few more minutes." He knew it was a lie; he still had several feet left to climb, and the soot only seemed to be getting harder.

"I've had enough of your laziness, boy," Smudge snarled. "I agreed that we'd be done by five. It's ten to five. Either you sweep this chimney in the next ten minutes, or you don't eat tonight!"

There was a sound from below, one that made Jack's blood run cold: the hiss of a flaring match.

"No!" Jack cried.

He peered between his cramped knees and saw it: the flicker of a yellow flame beneath him.

A moment later, thick, black smoke rolled into the chimney, seeing a way out. But this chimney had been badly blocked even before it had a child wedged into it. Now, the smoke had nowhere to go—except into Jack's eyes and lungs.

He cried out. "No! Please! No!"

"Sweep, boy!" Smudge roared. "You want fresh air? Then get to the top!"

Sobs overtook Jack. He couldn't hold them back; they wrenched from him, shaking his body as he frantically pounded the soot with his brush. The chunks came free with painful slowness as smoke and choking filled Jack's world. His screams became coughs, then screams again when the heat rose from the hearth, intense and blazing on his feet and buttocks. Soon, the bricks, too, were almost too hot to touch. Jack was being cooked alive.

"Stop screaming, boy. Sweep!" Smudge bellowed.

The brush slipped in Jack's sweaty hands. He barely kept his grasp as another cough wrenched through him. Desperate, he clawed at the soot with his fingers and only succeeded in tearing his nails.

"What is the meaning of this?" a posh voice thundered from below.

"Oh! Mr. Leeds, sir!" Smudge spluttered. "You're—you were only meant to be home at five-thirty."

"Are you mad, man?" the homeowner cried. "You're filling this house with smoke. Put that fire out at once!"

Pokers screamed below Jack, and wonderfully, blessedly, the heat reduced. He cowered in the chimney, sobbing, sweat and tears and saliva dripping from his chin as the roaring flames subsided.

"Is there a *child* in there?" Mr. Leeds demanded.

"Don't worry about him, sir. He's quite all right," said Smudge. "Just needed a little incentive to hurry up, that's all. We were hoping to get done on time, sir."

"No wonder it sounded like a banshee was stuffed into that chimney!" Mr. Leeds yelled. "Get him down now!"

"He's not finished yet, sir," Smudge began.

"I don't care!" Mr. Leeds thundered. "His wailing is upsetting my children. Now get him down!"

A long, seething pause followed.

"Jack," said Smudge, with forced calm, "get down."

Relief washed over Jack. He shimmied down and landed hard amid the ashes, burning his shoes. When he scrambled from the chimney, soot and ashes showered the rug.

He looked up at Mr. Leeds, hoping desperately for kindness, but it was a vain hope. The handsome, wealthy man's face twisted in utter revulsion and he recoiled from Jack.

"Look at this!" he roared at Smudge as if Jack wasn't present. "Look at the mess!" He indicated the soot all over the room and the smoke still hovering at the ceiling. "I employ you to clean my home, Mr. Blackwood, not to make it worse."

"Have you checked the other rooms, sir?" Smudge asked. "I can assure you that—"

Mr. Leeds held up a hand, silencing Smudge immediately. "I have no interest in any of your assurances." He produced a leather wallet from his pocket and handed Smudge several coins. "Please leave my premises at once."

"But sir, the chimney—" Smudge began.

"I think you've done enough," Mr. Leeds snapped. "What's more, I've never known such a useless sweep as you. Your children are always noisy and upsetting, and you always leave the house in filth. Do not expect me to engage your services in the future."

Smudge's jaw dropped. Jack slunk toward the door; mercifully, neither of the men seemed to notice him.

"Now take your money and go," said Mr. Leeds imperiously.

Smudge gripped the coins, then glanced at them. "Sir, this is not the amount we agreed on."

"You can be glad you're getting anything other than a demand to replace my carpets!" Mr. Leeds shouted.

Smudge ducked his head, anger and terror in his eyes. Jack knew better than to stay near such a combination. He turned tail and bolted for the courtyard outside, where Beryl was waiting, sobbing, terror on her little face. The other children murmured in sympathy; Beryl said nothing. She only gripped his hand, tight and trembling, like she would never let go.

"I'm sorry, everyone," said Larry. He sat in the middle of the ring of hungry children, opening a single, half-empty brown paper bag. "It's not much, but I suppose we're lucky to be getting dinner at all."

He extracted half a loaf of stale bread. Muffled cries of dismay came from the children; Jack had to press his lips together to keep himself from sobbing. Hunger made his arms and legs feel leaden.

"It's all because of Jack," said Mikey moodily. "He was the one who was too slow with that chimney."

"Don't say that!" Beryl sprang to her feet, fists clenched. "Jack did his best. You don't know what it was like in that chimney."

"Beryl's right." Larry made a placating gesture. "Sit down, Beryl. This is nobody's fault. This is just because of—" He stopped suddenly.

The children remained silent, eyes on the bread. Larry carefully tore it into roughly equal pieces and distributed it among the children. Jack scarfed his down in a few huge, hungry gulps. The stale bread burned his sore, inflamed throat on the way down.

"Because of what, Larry?" said Anna quietly. She was a little older than Jack.

Larry sighed.

"We know something's wrong," said Mikey. "Smudge is harsher than ever."

"And he's giving us less and less food," said Anna.

"It's because we're not so busy anymore, isn't it?" said Mikey. "We're not doing as many houses in a day anymore. People keep complaining to Smudge about us. They say we work too slowly and we look sick."

Jack blinked, surprised, and looked around the group of knock-kneed, pale-faced children. He supposed they did look sick.

Larry sighed. "It's true. Smudge has been losing business in the past few weeks and that means he has less money to buy food for himself… and for us."

"Food!" Anna scoffed. "As if he spends all his money on food. He's always buying nice new clothes and fancy things to put in his house. He doesn't care about *us*."

None of the children reacted to her words. They weren't news to them.

"What can we do?" said Jack quietly. "Do we need to work better?"

"I don't think we can, Jackie," said Larry. "I don't think it's us. How can we work better if we don't have enough to eat? Besides, it's about more than just our work."

"What, then?" Anna asked.

Larry shrugged. "People don't like children to be chimney sweeps anymore. People around here heard about Archie and didn't like it. Some people won't hire sweeps with little children at all. They say it's cruel."

Jack gazed down at his skinned knuckles and felt his burning lungs. He couldn't deny it, but where else was he meant to get food and shelter?

"What will we do, then?" Anna asked quietly.

"I don't know," said Larry. His jaw clenched. "But I'll think of something."

"Come on, Jack," said Beryl softly. "Let's go to sleep. I'm so tired."

They sipped their cups of water and then curled up on their soot sacks, very quiet. Beryl's knees pressed against Jack's back.

Every time he closed his eyes, he felt the heat of the flames in the chimney, felt the smoke choking his chest.

"We'll go to the farm someday," Beryl whispered. "Your mama's farm."

Jack tried to imagine it. In his mind's eye, there were fields and trees and a cool, clear stream to wash in anytime he wanted.

"Someday," he murmured.

Jack's eyes were so sore that he could barely keep them open. A gummy black discharge clung to the lashes, threatening to seal his eyelids closed. They itched, but rubbing them only made them hurt all the more.

"I'll help you wash them when we get home, Jack," Beryl whispered.

She gripped his hand tightly, the calluses hard on her tiny palm.

Jack nodded, miserable. He blinked the filminess away from his vision.

"They'll feel better in the morning," Larry encouraged him. "It's because we swept factory chimneys today. They're awful on the eyes."

"Hey!" Smudge yelled from ahead. "Be quiet!"

The children fell silent as they trudged down the street toward their home after another exhausting day.

Smudge unlocked the door and shoved it open, then hung back as Beryl and Jack led the way inside.

Mikey and Annie followed, then Larry, as always, brought up the rear. But before he could enter, Smudge grabbed his shoulder.

"No," he said. "Not you."

Larry stopped, confused. "Wh-what, Guv?"

"You stay out here," Smudge ordered.

Annie gasped. "What are you doing with Larry?"

"Go inside," Smudge commanded.

"No!" Annie cried. "What—"

"I said, go inside!" Smudge thundered.

Jack's heart hammered in horror. They stared at Larry in petrified silence. Jack didn't know what was about to happen, but his stomach knotted with terror, and Beryl clung to his hand with trembling, cold fingers.

"It's all right," said Larry, his words tight with tension. "It's all right. Go inside."

"But—" Annie began.

Smudge took a menacing step forward, and she screamed and darted inside. Mikey, Jack, and Beryl hurried after her.

Smudge slammed the door behind them, but his footsteps didn't go down the hallway. Instead, they heard him and Larry leaving the building.

"What's happening, Guv?" Larry asked.

"Shut up, boy," said Smudge.

Silence fell. Seconds trickled past, slow as syrup.

"I have to see what's happening," Annie whispered.

"Annie, no," said Mikey.

She ignored him and opened the door a tiny crack. Jack, Beryl, and Mikey crowded around the gap and peered outside.

Larry and Smudge stood on the pavement. Larry hugged himself in the cold; Smudge had his hands in the pockets of his thick jacket. Larry's eyes looked wide and white against his soot-stained face.

"Ah," said Smudge. "Here he is."

A sturdy figure strode down the sidewalk toward Smudge and Larry. The bow-legged man had massive arms and a tanned face with heavy lips that twisted down at the corners.

"Smudge!" he roared. "Is this the boy?"

"That's right," said Smudge. "Look at him!" He thumped Larry on the back, making him stagger. "He's big and strong. Clever, too. He'll make a perfect blacksmith's apprentice."

"What?" Annie gasped.

Mikey shushed her.

The blacksmith looked Larry up and down. "I don't know, Smudge. Sweeping ruins them. Does he have any cancer?"

"No, sir. None," said Smudge. "Do you, boy?"

"What do you want with me?" Larry asked.

Smudge cuffed him on the back of the head. "No lip from you!"

"You're coming to work for me as an apprentice," said the blacksmith. "Learn to forge iron and shoe horses."

He turned to Smudge. "I'll take him, but three shillings is absurd for a skinny mite like this. He'll need feeding before he can handle big horses."

"Three shillings is a bargain," Smudge scoffed.

"I can get them cheaper at the workhouse," said the blacksmith, "and I shall, if you're not interested in taking two shillings and sixpence."

Smudge's muscles tensed. "Fine," he growled.

The blacksmith dropped coins into Smudge's hand.

"Wait. Wait, no." Larry backed away. "I... I can't go with him. What about the others? They need me!"

"Forget them, boy." The blacksmith grabbed his arm. "You'll have a better life working with me."

"No," Annie moaned. "Larry!"

"Shhhh!" Mikey grabbed her left arm, and Beryl and Jack grabbed her right. They towed her back into the room as Smudge's footsteps entered the hallway. Larry's protests faded into the distance as the four remaining sweep children huddled on the floor, wide-eyed and scared. Annie tried to swallow her sobs.

The door crashed open. Smudge tossed a sack onto the floor between them.

"One less mouth to feed," he snapped. "Work well tomorrow or you'll be the next to go."

He slammed the door so hard that wood splinters fell to the ground.

Chapter Three

Jack's head felt like a lump of lead attached to his neck. He sat with his knees to his chest, arms wrapped around his knees, head resting on them as the headache pounded away behind his eyes. He'd stopped feeling hunger yesterday—their second day without any food. Now, numb weakness soaked into his muscles.

He summoned the strength to look up as Annie and Mikey trooped back into the room. Empty sacks lined the floor; there were no more full ones to use as pillows.

"I can't believe there were only two sacks to sell today," Annie moaned.

"That's because we've only swept two houses all week." Mikey sagged to the ground as though he felt as weak as Jack.

Annie held her head in her hands. "Do you think we'll ever eat again?"

Jack stared at the corner where Beryl lay. She slept, hands folded under her head, knees drawn up to her chest.

Her little hands were pale and bony, her wrists stick-thin where they protruded from her sleeves. She looked more like a walking skeleton than a child.

"It's been weeks since we ate every night," Mikey murmured. "Smudge tried to sell me yesterday."

"What?" Annie gasped. "He did?"

"Yes, to a tailor, but he said I was too skinny." Mikey swallowed. "Smudge said he would take us all to the workhouse if we didn't work harder."

"How are we meant to work if we're so hungry we can barely move?" Annie cried.

Workhouse. The word slammed through Jack, heavy and leaden. He hugged his knees tighter and squeezed his eyes shut. They separated boys and girls in the workhouse. If Smudge took them there, he might never see Beryl again, just as he'd never seen Mama again.

The door creaked, and all the children tensed. Mikey sprang to his feet, swayed a moment, then steadied.

"Ready to go, Guv," he said quickly.

Smudge sneered. "Only tomorrow. The Readings have booked us for the day. I expect your best work, understand?"

"Yes, Guv." Mikey hung his head.

Smudge slammed a pot down in the middle of the floor. "Eat. But you'd better show me something tomorrow for this investment."

The smell of food rolled through the room. Beryl sat up with a gasp. Jack clutched her arm as Mikey and Annie crowded the pot, which was half full of watery gruel.

"Here. Quickly." Mikey grabbed four tin spoons from a shelf. "Let's eat before it gets cold."

Jack thrust a spoon into Beryl's hand. She stumbled to the pot and gulped down a spoonful, not caring how scalding the gruel was. Jack sat beside her, and the room filled with the desperate sounds of gulping and smacking lips as the children slurped down the scraps of food.

Looking at Beryl's bony hands and pinched cheekbones, Jack could only hope that it would be enough.

The smell of the fresh bread drifted down the street in an aromatic cloud. Jack's mouth watered as he followed Annie and Mikey toward their building. Beryl stumbled along beside him, brush on her shoulder, eyes listless. The gruel had been yesterday; they'd eaten nothing that day. It felt like an eternity.

Now, though, things would change. They'd done good work at the latest house; the owner had paid them a little extra. Smudge led the way down the street with a spring in his step. He carried that gorgeous golden loaf of fresh bread under his arm, and Jack couldn't take his eyes off the magnificent object.

He could imagine how wonderful that fresh, fluffy bread would taste. Warm and soothing and soft. His mouth watered, and the anticipation was almost enough to make him forget about his burning eyes or his sore back and shoulders.

"My feet," Beryl whimpered, tears shimmering in her eyes. She limped with exhaustion.

"Almost there, Beryl." Jack squeezed her hand. "Almost there. Then we'll eat."

The streets were dark and silent around them as Smudge strode to the front door.

They'd finished late; they'd been lucky to find a baker desperate enough to sell anything at this time of night. In silence, they stood hungrily waiting and watching the loaf as Smudge pushed the door to their room open.

"Put the sacks by the door," Smudge ordered. "The farmer's coming in the morning. Once he's paid for it, you'll get your breakfast."

Mikey froze with a soot sack balanced on his shoulders.

"Wh-what about tonight?" Annie cried.

Jack's heart swooped into his boots. Beryl whimpered.

"A little hunger won't kill you," Smudge snapped. With that, he strode into his own tenement and slammed the door.

Mikey dropped the sack onto the ground and then sagged down on top of it with his head in his hands.

"No," Annie moaned. "But... but why? He has food... he has more than enough. Why won't he give us any?"

"We'll eat in the morning," said Jack, trying not to feel as though his heart had fallen through the floor. "He'll give us something at breakfast, he said he would."

Annie sobbed quietly. Jack and Beryl stumbled into the room, and Mikey pushed the door shut, then curled up on his side and simply lay there.

Beryl sank onto a pile of sacks and stared at nothing. Tears flowed silently over her cheeks.

"I know you're hungry," Jack mumbled. He, too, felt like a hole had been gnawed in his belly.

Beryl said nothing. She simply stared at him with frighteningly hollow eyes, then rolled onto her side and lay there, crying quietly.

Jack curled up beside her as darkness fell. Annie's sobs faded to snores. Even Mikey dropped off to sleep. But poor little Beryl never stopped weeping. Every time her little shoulders finally stilled and Jack thought she'd gone to sleep, she would startle awake, and the quiet crying would begin again.

He knew her hunger; he felt it in his own belly, in his own bones. It felt as though his own body was eating itself alive. As the night dragged on, Jack's heart and body both screamed for solace. Beryl's crying continued unabated.

They were alone and starving while Smudge had a full loaf of delicious, fresh bread all to himself.

The church bell had struck one in the morning when Jack could no longer take it. As soon as Beryl slipped into a half sleep again, he rolled to his knees, his plan fully formed. He knew what he wanted to do was wrong on some level, but nothing could be more wrong than what he and the others were suffering.

Quietly, he slipped through their door and into the hallway. His tiny, sooty feet were almost silent on the floorboards; around him, nothing stirred but for the quiet creaking of the elderly building in the wind.

On tiptoe, Jack edged to Smudge's door and peered through the keyhole. He had only seen glimpses of Smudge's tenement before, but it was enough to know that the kitchen was at the front, with cupboards on the walls and a table and chairs in the middle.

He guessed that the bread might be on the table. Either way, it had to be in the kitchen. He knew he could reach it.

As quietly as he could, Jack gripped the door handle and pulled. By some miracle, it wasn't locked; perhaps Smudge had been too hungry and hasty to lock it. It swung open with the softest of creaks, and Jack left it that way as he tiptoed into the kitchen.

A sliver of light from an upstairs gas lamp made it through the boards forming the ceiling above, and with its help, Jack spotted the bread. It lay on the table, a knife beside it. Smudge had only eaten half of the loaf.

There was plenty of food left for the children.

Jack edged across the room and stood on tiptoe to reach for the bread. He felt the wonderful, springy texture between his fingers and pulled it toward him, and the bread knife tipped off the table and clattered to the floor at his feet, the loudest sound he'd ever heard.

"Hey!" Smudge roared from inside.

Jack yanked the bread down and jammed it under his arm. He bolted for the door, but he wasn't quick enough. A huge hand closed on his free arm and yanked him back, sending the precious loaf tumbling to the ground.

"No!" The strangled yelp wrenched from Jack's throat.

"Thief!" Smudge bellowed. "You little thief! You ungrateful, wretched, disgusting little thief!"

His yank pulled Jack clean off his feet. He landed hard on his backside, the bones meeting the floor with a thud that reverberated to his neck and jaw. Jack burst out with a cry of pain and terror.

Jack's eyes never left the splendid bread loaf lying on the ground, smeared now with dust from Smudge's floor. He lunged to his feet and stretched a panicking arm toward it, and Smudge slapped his hand away with stinging force.

"Thief!" he roared. "You should be hanged!"

Anger and pain surged through Jack. He stumbled to his feet and rounded on Smudge, who towered over him, huge and looming and reeking.

"We're only children!" Jack cried. "We're so hungry. Please. Please!"

Smudge's quick cuff landed on the back of Jack's head with burning intensity.

"Silence, you criminal," he roared.

"Sir!" Beryl stumbled through the open front door. Annie and Mikey were right behind her; she wrenched from Annie's hands and ran a few feet across the floor toward them. "Please, don't hurt him. He was only trying to help us." Tears sparkled on her cheeks. "We're all so hungry."

"Be quiet!" Smudge bellowed.

He grasped his cane from its hook by the door and turned to Jack. "Be ready for the beating of your life, boy," he snarled.

"Guv, please," Mikey begged.

Smudge gesticulated with the cane. "Silence!"

The other children watched in mute horror as Smudge strode to Jack. Without ceremony, he grabbed Jack by the back of his shirt, fell into a chair at the table, and hauled Jack's wriggling, helpless body over his lap. Jack cried out, grasping at nothing, but he was powerless against the strong sweep. Smudge ripped his coat and shirt upward to expose his back and landed the first blow of the cane squarely over his protruding spine.

Jack gritted his teeth over his scream of agony. At first, he was defiant and furious. But when the third and the fourth blows landed on his cold flesh, his defiance gave way to sobbing in agony, begging for mercy. Mercy did not come. Smudge struck him another three times, then shoved him to the ground. Jack landed on his hands and knees, trembling and sobbing.

"Be grateful I don't give you to the bobbies, boy," he hissed. "Now get out of my house."

He turned and strode from the room.

"J-Jack." Beryl stuttered his name.

Jack raised his head, sobbing with pain and fright. The little girl stood a few feet away, clutching in her hands the smooth, white bread. Crumbs dusted her lips.

"Here," she whispered, extending a chunk of bread toward him.

Mikey and Annie ate in hungry gasps, but pain made Jack's stomach heave with nausea.

"Go away," he snapped.

Tears filled Beryl's eyes. "Please," she croaked.

"Go away!" Jack screamed. He stumbled to his feet in a swirl of pain and terror. "I did this for you!"

Beryl stumbled back, wide-eyed, her mouth dropping open.

Jack hurt. His back screamed with every breath; terror and hunger surged through him. He didn't know how to stop hurting except to scream, to let the pain out, to make someone else feel as he felt.

"If you weren't here, this would never have happened!" he shrieked.

Annie and Mikey barely noticed his screaming; they were too busy tearing the loaf apart, scarfing down the bread for which he'd been beaten. Rage and pain made his vision red.

"I'm sorry, Jackie," Beryl sobbed. "I'm so sorry. I'm so sorry. I'm so sorry." She wailed as she pushed the remaining bread toward him, crumbling between her fingers. "Take it all."

"I don't want it," Jack screamed. He slapped her hands away.

Beryl collapsed to the ground, sobbing. "I'm so sorry, Jackie!"

He stared at her, knowing he'd hurt her, and the weight of his emotions felt like a whirlwind trapped in his chest.

This was a place of absolute pain. Everything hurt; his heart, his body, his poor, throbbing head.

He would wish, later, that he could say that his mind emptied completely of coherent thought. That his next act was one of pure, animal instinct. But it was not. The truth was that he looked into Beryl's eyes and wanted to harm her as he perceived that she had harmed him.

"I hate you!" he screamed. "I hate all of you!"

Then he turned and bolted from the place of pain, unable to face what he'd done, what had been done to him.

"Jackie!" Beryl's wail followed him down the hallway and out into the street.

He didn't slow down. He kept his head low and sprinted away as fast as his aching legs could carry him. There was no plan, no decision; all he knew was that he had to get as far away from Smudge as he could, and never be hurt like this again.

Jack ran until his legs would bear him no longer. Then he collapsed in an alley, sobbing with pain, wheezing with exertion. No longer caring about his fate, he wrapped his arms around himself and curled into a corner until he fell asleep on the cold, hard stone.

Had the wind always been this cold?

It must have been. Jack struggled to keep his sore eyes open as he huddled on the pavement, sheltering beneath the broad wheel of a farmer's wagon on the market square's corner. He'd stumbled across the market square the day before... yesterday morning. It felt like a thousand years ago. The smells of food had enticed him here, and now they kept him here, though he'd tasted precious little of it.

Perhaps the wind had always sliced like a thousand tiny knives pricking his skin. He must have felt it walking from the tenement to the houses where he worked, or perched on a rooftop, waiting for Smudge to put the ladder up.

But ever since running from the tenement, the wind felt different. Jack closed his eyes, leaning against the wheel for a moment's respite. It was because there was no reprieve, he was sure. Horrid as climbing chimneys was, smelly and sooty as their tenement had been, Jack had never in his life slept outside in the cold alone. He'd spent a couple of nights on the streets with Mama, perhaps, before the workhouse; but all he remembered was her arms around him and his face cuddled into her chest.

This was different. So appallingly different.

"Hey!" someone barked. "Move!"

Jack sprang to his feet and scrambled aside before his eyes could open. A heavyset man brushed past him, sneered, and mounted the wagon.

"Please, Guv." Jack extended a trembling hand, his naked fingertips nipped red beyond his threadbare, fingerless gloves. "Spare a penny?"

The man scoffed and whipped his horse, which charged off with a snort.

Without the wheel's meagre shelter, the wind was harsher than ever. Jack dug his hands into his pocket and sloped off miserably to his only other spot of shelter—a corner between a stall selling dried fish and a barber shop.

The wind still sliced from the north, but it was better than standing around in the cold.

His belly rumbled; he was startled to find that it still could. Apart from a few bits of bread crusts he'd picked from a garbage heap yesterday morning, he hadn't eaten in days.

The old man who ran the dried fish stall was too busy crying his wares to the threadbare crowd to notice Jack. Most of the people here were shabby housewives with pinched faces who counted every penny before they bought bread, fruit, or scraps of meat. One haggled with the stall keeper now, trying to get a penny off the price of a piece of fish. Jack tucked himself into his corner, knees to his chest, shivering in the cold.

The stall keeper finally cut a piece off the fish and sold the rest to the mollified housewife. He sighed as he stared at the piece of fish in his hand. Jack stared at it, too, hardly knowing he was doing it. Staring at food he'd never get to eat had become a habit.

"Only cut it off because she was so rude," the stall keeper grunted. "Here, kid."

He tossed the fish toward Jack, who caught it mid-air and shoved it into his mouth. The oily goodness flooded his senses, and he grunted with pleasure as he choked down bites of fish.

"Starving, aren't you?" the stall keeper observed.

Jack didn't stop chewing. His world was nothing but this mouthful of food.

"Covered in soot. Aren't you a sweep's lad?" the stall keeper asked.

Jack looked away.

"A runaway." The stall keeper sighed. "Heaven knows nobody can blame you, but if you want my advice, lad, go on back to your master. Beg him to take you back. Winter ain't kind to anyone on these streets."

Jack ate his fish in silence, gazing down the street. How far had he run the night he'd fled Smudge? Blocks? Miles? He had no way of knowing. He couldn't read the street signs; he didn't know the tenement's address.

Even if he wanted to go back, he couldn't.

Misery turned his last mouthfuls to sand. He swallowed them down without an appetite as his belly protested at the rich food. Closing his eyes, Jack fought the nausea, determined not to lose this lucky meal.

Again, Beryl's scream echoed through his mind. *"Jackie!"*

He knew he'd never forget the tears in her eyes as he'd yelled the words that he knew weren't true: *"I hate you, I hate you!"*

They resounded through his heart now, accompanied by Beryl's sobs, and Jack squeezed his eyelids to hold back his tears.

"I'm sorry, Beryl," he whispered. "I'm sorry."

The wind whipped his words away and blew them to scattered pieces across the market square.

Part Two

Chapter Four

Two Years Later

Jack's belly was empty, but he whistled as he walked. He tried to ignore the crick in his neck from sleeping crammed into the doorway of an abandoned warehouse, trying to avoid the bad sorts that roamed these streets at night. He'd lost his left big toe to frostbite during that first brutal winter on the streets and sometimes the stump still ached in the cold—like this morning.

But Jack was alive, and he knew where to find food, and he hadn't lost any toes this winter. Spring was coming. Besides, people seldom liked beggars with long faces, he'd learned. They preferred them to be charming and cheerful, provided they still had dirty faces and pinched features. This much was easy.

Jack paused at the edge of the market square. He was miles away from the place where the kindly stall keeper had given him a piece of fish nearly two years ago; the bobbies there had driven him off a few months before.

It had proven to be a blessing in disguise. This square was larger, cleaner, and brighter, with storefronts instead of stalls, their wooden signs swinging gently in the rising wind.

He pulled his collar up to his jaw; its baggy length hung below his knees. Straightening his cap on his head, Jack glanced around the thickening crowd that always gathered here in the mornings. These housewives had rosy cheeks and plump bodies with their aprons tied tight in the middle of their backs. They held shopping lists and carried baskets.

They often had a few pennies to spare for a friendly beggar.

A regular strode down the pavement opposite Jack now, her basket of fruit and vegetables hanging from her arm. His eyes narrowed as she approached the road's crossing. The mire of morning traffic was trampled into the cobbles: road apples, dust, and miscellaneous grime. The woman glanced at her polished shoes and hesitated.

A shadow detached itself from a nearby corner, brandishing a broom.

"Mornin', m'lady!" the crossing-sweeper chirped.

The woman smiled. "Good morning."

"Let me help you there." The crossing-sweeper tweaked his threadbare cap and got to work.

He moved swiftly over the crossing ahead of the woman, sweeping aside the dust, manure and debris. The woman smiled as she strode over the cobbles with no filth to impede her way.

Jack didn't think of the fact that he often slept in similar filth; a manure heap near a livery stable close by had become his bed. Instead, he kept his gaze on the broom as it worked over the cobbles, teasing filth from between the stones.

They reached the other side, and the woman tucked a hand into her purse and slipped a whole sixpence into the sweeper's hand. A sixpence was enough to buy a day's food in Jack's world.

"Thank you kindly," she said.

The sweeper beamed and tweaked his cap again. "Anytime, m'lady."

He turned and looked around for his next customer, broom ready in his hands. The woman strode toward Jack, who gave his most winning smile as he extended a hand toward her. "Spare a penny for a hungry boy, m'lady?"

The word didn't have the same effect on her when spoken by an eight-year-old beggar instead of a helpful crossing sweeper. She gave him a pitying glance, then handed him a farthing before striding away.

Jack stared at the tiny coin in his hand, then looked up at the crossing-sweeper. The broom he carried cost seven pence. A shop across the square sold them; Jack had stared at them in the window many a time. As the sweeper stepped out in front of a handsome man with polished shoes, chattering merrily to pass the time, Jack knew that a broom would be his ticket to easier meals.

He gently placed the farthing in his pocket, feeling the other coins there. On the few occasions when he'd had enough money to eat more than once a day, Jack had forced himself to keep the coins set aside instead. He had five whole pennies now. Only two more to go if he wanted that broom.

Determination flooded him, and Jack strode toward the opposite corner, where the crowd was thickest around the grocer's shop and a sweatshop filled with clothing. He took his usual position under a streetlamp, allowing the warm golden light to bathe him with a kinder glow than the pale dawn, and smiled as widely as he could as a knot of young women strode past.

"Top of the morning to you, m'ladies!" he called. "Beautiful day. I do love your flowers, miss."

One of the young women chuckled and touched the red flower in her hair. "Aren't you a cheerful little thing," she said.

"Sorrow don't get us nowhere, miss," said Jack. He extended a grubby hand. "Spare a ha'penny for a little lad?"

"Oh, he's so sweet, Doris," said her companion. "Do give him something."

"I suppose it can't hurt. It's a pity seeing such a dear little thing on the street." The woman fished in her purse. "Where are your parents, dear?"

The question was always a knife in Jack's heart. "Long gone, miss," he said. It was a better answer than the truth: that he didn't know, that he could only hope Mama would come to find him someday. "I still dream of my mama sometimes," he added. That much was true.

"Oh, you poor thing." The woman sighed as she dropped a penny into his hands. "Good luck to you."

She strode away, and Jack slipped the penny quickly into his pocket. Sixpence. He'd need something to buy food for today, but it was a promising start to the morning. Maybe he'd be able to squirrel away a penny or a farthing before the day was up.

If he could get a broom and earn a little more money, then perhaps he could afford a box to sleep in. Maybe even nicer clothes, later, and admission to a bathhouse. Then he might get a job.

It could change everything for him, if—

"Hey, boy," someone growled.

Jack forced himself not to jump. He turned with his bravest smile, hand clenching over the few coins in his pocket, hoping to charm a grumpy shopkeeper into giving him a scrap of bread or some offcut fabric to use as a blanket.

But it was no shopkeeper who stood behind him. Instead, three beggars glared at him, their clothes even more ragged than his own. The woman's skirt hung in tatters around her bare, bony calves. She wore work boots several sizes too big. Behind her, two men loomed, showing off broken teeth and empty eyes.

"You don't belong here," the woman hissed.

Jack stepped back. "I don't know what you mean." He glanced up and down the street, wanting to flee, and his stomach lurched when he saw two more beggars emerging from alleyways beside the shops. They circled around, blocking his escape.

"You know full well," the woman snarled. "Look at us! Old and ugly. Decrepit and smelly. How are we supposed to compete with *this*?"

She gestured at him angrily, and Jack caught sight of his appearance in a shop window's reflection. His face was pale and grimy, but his mop of curls fell endearingly over large, soft eyes.

"You're taking our money, boy," the man behind her growled.

Jack swallowed. "I—I've never stolen from you."

"Yes, you have," the woman hissed. "You do every day. You take and you take. Every time someone gives you a penny, it's one they might have given us."

"You need to leave this square," a man added.

"Yes." The woman's eyes narrowed. "This is our patch."

Jack stepped back and bumped into a bony man, who clutched at his coat with skeleton fingers. He cried out and stumbled away, almost crashing into the woman, who grabbed his thin arms in cold, hard claws.

"Leave, boy," she hissed, "or I'll kill you."

Jack stared into her yellow eyes and utterly believed her.

"Now give me that penny," she hissed.

Jack hesitated. She didn't know he had other money with him. He opened his hand, trying to drop all of his coins except the penny, and they jingled noisily into his pocket.

"He's got more!" one of the men wailed.

"Get it!" the woman shrieked.

Jack screamed as she wrenched his hands away from his pockets. His penny tumbled from his fingers and jingled on the ground; someone swiped it within a heartbeat. Hands plunged into his coat and trouser pockets, groping, searching, unfeeling. In seconds, his hard-earned pennies were all gone.

"Now go!" The woman shoved him so that he fell on his hands and knees. "Run away, boy, or I'll kill you!"

Again, her raspy tone told him that she meant it. Jack stumbled to his feet and ran for his life.

Rain poured past the shop's overhang in a grey sheet.

Everything was grey in this part of the city. The grimy walls. The streaks of smog rising against the low clouds. The sluggish water of a tributary running past the square. The raindrops on the iron railings bordering the dirty water.

The faces of the people who hurried past, pinched and pale, none of them sparing Jack even a second glance.

He'd run as far as he could from the square where the other beggars had cornered him, terrified of the woman who'd threatened to kill him. He knew she'd have done if it she could catch him. But now he was in a part of the city that felt as miserable and skeletal as the tired old donkey plodding past, drawing a rag-and-bone cart, its mad old owner cackling at nothing.

A little boy dashed across the road and tried to snatch the rag-and-bone man's purse from his cart. The old man grabbed the cart and cackled, and the boy vanished into an alley.

No one paid the attempted theft any mind. Though the street was packed, no one seemed to look past their destination: they all stared straight ahead and hurried on, ignoring Jack no matter how high-pitched his plea.

It had been three days since he'd fled the market square. Three long, cold, rainy days without a morsel of food to pass his lips. He'd drunk from his hands in the disgusting river. The bobbies here kept undesirables away from the only pump, and Jack, it seemed, was as undesirable as could be here.

Now, he felt almost too weak to extend his hand to a passer-by. He stared up at them in mute plea instead; a plea that went entirely unheard. Arms wrapped around himself, he shivered, droplets splashing him from the gutter where it poured into the street a few feet away. But if he moved up, the shop owner would see him from the window and chase him off. He'd learned that lesson the hard way.

A portly man strode past, his buttons straining over his belly. Jack stared enviously at the broad expanse. The pure silver chain of a pocket watch dangled from his pocket, and the man pulled the watch out and glanced at it.

He'd seen pocket watches in windows with numbers next to them. Jack wasn't good at numbers, but he knew that pocket watches were bought in pounds instead of pennies. Anyone who had a whole pound had enough to eat. What more could they want?

"Please, sir," he croaked, extending a hand. "Spare a penny."

"Go to the workhouse, boy," the man snapped, and hurried away.

Jack leaned his head against the wall and stared at nothing as hunger gnawed at his bones. What now? How long did it take to starve to death?

The longest he'd gone without food was four days. He didn't think it was possible to go much longer with collapsing.

Shadows across the street caught his eye. He spotted three children approaching the bakery across the way. One loitered by the door, whistling casually as he gazed through the window. The child's coat was too big for him, and had been mended, but it seemed warm and sturdy. Envy shot through Jack at the sight.

The other two children approached the front door and stepped inside. The baker turned to them, and the second he did so, the little boy outside reached in and snatched three loaves of bread from the baskets in the window. He moved with breathtaking speed; one second he was outside, the next he was sprinting down the sidewalk, bread under his arms.

"Hey!" the shopkeeper roared. "Stop! Thief!"

The other two children scattered in different directions. The baker stumbled outside, looking left and right, but somehow all three had already vanished into the crowd. Even Jack couldn't spot them.

The whole thing had taken less than a minute. A minute's work, for three loaves of bread! It seemed impossible.

Jack blinked. *Three loaves of bread*. Those children would all have more than they could eat now, and it had been so quick and so very, very easy.

Hunger drew him to his feet. He drifted across the road and stood outside the bakery, staring at the loaves within. The baker gesticulated angrily from behind the counter and Jack decided to wander in a different direction instead. His heart pounded as he moved among the crowd, invisible to them. They bumped against him, watch chains jingling.

Watch chains. Watches. *Pounds*. How much food could you buy with a pound? Perhaps enough to fill Jack's starving belly.

It was a simple solution, so very simple. He glanced around and saw no bobbies, so he kept his head low and moved a little nearer to a man whose brass pocket watch bumped carelessly around in the hip pocket of his coat. Jack's hands were small and quick, and he reached inside and grabbed it with an ease that startled him, then thrust it into his own pocket.

His heart hammered, but nothing happened. No one turned to look. He ducked his head low and moved away quickly, like he'd seen other pickpockets do in his two years on the streets, and that was that.

He darted back to his spot beside the store and hunched down, suddenly no longer feeling the cold rain that soaked through his clothes. With a thundering heart, he withdrew the brass watch from his pocket and kept it cupped in his hands so that no one could see as he stared at it. It ticked along cheerfully, the little hands moving over a face that made no sense to him, but that hardly mattered.

Pounds, Jack thought.

In the end, it turned out that stolen watches weren't worth pounds like Jack had hoped. The man behind the counter in the grimy pawnshop down the street turned it over in his hands, frowning.

"Where did you say you got this?" he grumbled.

Jack glanced around the display cases surrounding him, suddenly nervous. Watches, rings, cigar cases, and expensive silver purses lay in the cases. He wondered if they'd all been honestly come by.

"I found it, Guv," he said.

The pawnbroker eyed Jack, then the watch. Then he shrugged as if it didn't matter to him either way.

"I'll give you a shilling," he said.

Jack's heart flipped. An entire shilling? Twelve whole pennies? It was more money than he'd ever held in his hands in his life. The fact that it was less than he'd dreamed of hardly mattered. It almost didn't feel real.

"Oh, yes, Guv," he burst out.

"Good." The pawnbroker tossed him the precious coin.

Jack grabbed it out of the air and hugged it to his chest, then turned and fled the pawnshop before anyone could stop him. He ran as fast as he could to the bakery where the children had stolen bread moments before. The baker tensed when he crashed through the door.

"Go away!" he barked, reaching for a broom to use as a weapon. "I don't need—"

"I have a shilling!" Jack yelled, slapping it on the counter. "Please. I need bread. Lots of bread."

The baker blinked at the coin, then at Jack, and softened slightly. "Two loaves?" he asked.

Jack eagerly nodded. The baker slipped two steaming loaves into a paper bag and handed them to him, then added a few more coins.

"What's this, Guv?" Jack asked.

"Your change, boy," said the baker.

Change? He could eat all he liked *and* have money left over? It all seemed incredible. Jack left the bakery skipping as he tore chunks from the first loaf with his teeth.

It was the best day of his life.

It was raining again, but this time, Jack didn't care. He lay easily on his back in the upper window of an abandoned warehouse—a space he'd secured by paying two pennies to the frightening old man who lived on the floor below. His new blanket rustled underneath him, cushioning him against the splintered floor, and he propped his head up on one hand as he ate a fresh green apple.

The rain pattered through the ruined roof in many places, plinking and plopping as it fell through the building. It poured down in a sheet beyond the small window through which Jack gazed at the street below, but his little spot was warm and dry. He'd forgotten how it felt to sleep wrapped in a blanket with a real roof over his head.

Carefully, he ate the apple core, leaving only the stick behind. Then he wiped his mouth and licked his fingers, allowing none of the apple juice to go to waste.

Tuppence for bread, tuppence for "rent", a penny for the apple he'd eaten for breakfast. After a little light begging yesterday, Jack had seven whole pennies left in his pocket, and he knew exactly what he could do with them. He could buy a broom and become a crossing-sweeper.

He thought of the crossing nearest the bakery. There were plenty of well-to-do folks there—folks who might need a crossing swept for them lest they dirty their pretty little shoes. He could buy a broom from the store across the road and get to work right away; they'd soon pay him something, and he could eat tonight. Twice in one day! It was almost unheard-of in Jack's life.

Then again...

Jack gazed at the crowd bustling below, the crowd who had so often passed him when he was hungry and desperate, sparing him not a second glance, let alone a penny for food. They carried their pocket-watches and their purses and didn't think of a boy who had nothing.

Would he rather sweep their streets, or pick their pockets?

He rolled up his blanket and stowed it in a corner, then left the warehouse quickly and quietly; the scary old man lay snoring in a corner, smelling of stale beer. Jack stepped into the rain, keeping his head down, and hurried down the sidewalk to the store that sold the brooms. He could see them from the window, and he stood there for a while, gazing at them. Thinking of how it felt to have a hard, wooden shaft in his hands, to push it over an unyielding surface, all for someone who wouldn't have the courtesy to ask his name.

It had been so easy to grasp that watch from the fat man's pocket the day before.

A strange twinge ran through his belly. He remembered Mama's laughter, her gentle eyes. Somehow, it felt as though she wouldn't like what he was doing.

Then again, Mama had loved him. She'd want him to do whatever he needed to stay alive.

Jack turned away and blended into the crowd. It was only seconds before he spotted a young woman prancing by with her basket on her shoulder, coins clinking in the corner. Slipping his hand inside and grabbing a sixpence was as easy as breathing, and in minutes, Jack was in the bakery again, buying bread.

He returned to his warehouse a few minutes later and lay back on his blanket, listening to the rain as he filled his mouth with great chunks of hot, sweet bread. And he forgot all about the possibility of a broom.

Jack walked with his arms swinging, shoulders back, head up. It was the first time in years that he could appreciate the day's sunshine for more than its mere warmth; he had a blanket and a coat waiting for him in his spot in the warehouse should the day turn cold. Now, he strolled about in a hole-ridden sweater that had cost him only two days' pickpocketing to obtain.

He pretended to gaze at the sunshine as it sparkled on the damp world, reflecting on puddles and caressing the smooth lines of the wrought-iron streetlights.

Around him, the crowd was no longer anonymous with umbrellas, hats, and scarves. Instead they laughed and talked as they strode along the street, yet they were still just as distracted as when they hurried through the rain. Now, they looked around at each other and the shops and the handsome horses and carriages rattling down the street instead of minding their pockets.

It was all the same to Jack. He eased himself into the thickest crowd on the sidewalk, a group of young men and women all happily strolling along with flowers in their buttonholes and ribbons in their hair. Anyone who could afford flowers and ribbons would be sure to have something worth picking in their pockets.

Jack quickly spotted the gleam of a silver cigar case protruding from the unguarded coat pocket of a young gentleman on his left. When the gentleman threw back his head to laugh at a comment his lady companion had made, Jack moved in. His little hand slipped in and out of the gentleman's pocket so swiftly that he felt nothing. Jack stayed with the crowd a little longer, then darted down an alleyway. When the group turned the corner at the street's end, the young man still hadn't noticed that Jack had taken his cigar case.

Jack leaned against the alley wall, admiring the little silver case. It had an inscription on the front; Jack thought the flowing script looked fancy, but couldn't read any of it. It hardly mattered. The pawnbroker would still give him a shilling or two for it.

He tucked it snugly into his coat and stepped out of the alley, and a rough pair of hands grabbed him by the shoulders. A feral, snarling face—crooked teeth, rampant freckles, and an eruption of red curls—eclipsed his vision. Before Jack could cry out, the apparition muscled him into the alley and pinned him up against the walls.

"Search him, boys!"

He'd expected a man's deep snarl, but instead heard the high-pitched tones of a young girl. Two small children—not much bigger than he—appeared on either side of him. They rifled through Jack's pockets with startling efficiency and came up with the cigar case and a sixpence.

"Hey!" Jack cried, kicking out. "That's mine! I'll call the bobbies, I will! You're stealing!"

"We're stealing?" The girl cackled, her grip tightening on his arms. She was stronger than she looked, and her foul breath was inches from her face, making him cringe.

"You'll call the bobbies, will you? Well then, what if we tell them what you do every day, you cheeky little mite?"

Jack's heart froze. He stared at the girl, heart pounding, as the two smaller children tugged and squealed over the cigar case.

"You listen to me, boy." The girl leaned closer. "I'm Liz Addleby, and this is my patch, do you hear me? *My patch*. No one pickpockets here but me and the kids. Do you hear me?"

Jack stared at her.

"Or else Finn might have something to say," Liz added in a low hiss.

She jerked her head to the right, and Jack followed the motion to a tall, lanky boy with pale skin and gangly limbs. His thatch of blond hair was so pale it was nearly white. Finn clenched his fists, a mean glint in his green eyes, and swung an arm. His fist landed in Jack's belly with shocking force, doubling him over. Tears of pain filled his eyes as he wheezed.

"Do you hear me?" Liz added.

"Yes," Jack whimpered. "Yes."

Liz released him. He fell to the grimy alley floor on his hands and knees, spluttering.

"Now run, boy," Liz snarled. "Run, and don't ever come back!"

Jack scrambled to his feet. He stared at the two smaller children—one now triumphantly held up the cigar case—and his gaze rested on Finn's cruel eyes. A gasp of fright escaped Jack, and he sprinted into the crowd.

But this time, he didn't flee. He ran without slowing down until he reached his warehouse and then huddled in the window, wrapped in his blanket and shaking, as he watched Liz's bright red head moving down the street with Finn and the other two close behind her. She pickpocketed as she walked with casual ease.

Jack's belly burned where Finn had hit him, but he clenched his little fists. First the terrifying beggars, now these kids. Finn hit hard—but Jack was sure he could outrun him.

"This is my patch, too," he whispered to the sunny day.

Chapter Five

The church bell struck seven as Jack loitered in the doorway of his abandoned warehouse. The scary old man's saw-like snores rose from the room behind him; for once, he was passed out drunk, and Jack could stay in the doorway a few moments without arousing his wrath. He took the opportunity to scan the street before him, careful as ever.

In the two weeks since Liz and the others had cornered him in the alley, Jack had learned their ways. They often avoided this part of the street in the early mornings, preferring to start on the other end. But often people passed this way as they headed to work this early in the morning.

They were leaner pickings than the midmorning shoppers, but Jack knew how to work this crowd; he knew what time the bobbies came by, and he knew what distracted them.

The church bell struck a quarter past seven. It was the perfect time. There would no police and no Liz, and Jack could work in peace.

He strolled from the warehouse door, whistling jovially in tune with a group of factory-worker children who hurried past him, their little tune trying to lift the weight of hearts made weary from endless work and harsh mistreatment. He paid the children no mind; they would have nothing anyway, their parents took it all. But just ahead was a group of factory men who wore thick coats and scarves and looked eagerly toward the bakery as they approached it. They'd be ready for breakfast, and they'd have the money for it.

Jack darted from one to the other, unnoticed in the thick crowd. He picked a penny here, tuppence there. One unwary worker was foolish enough to leave a whole sixpence in his coat pocket. Jack lifted it with a quick gleam of copper and dropped it into his own pocket, then rejoined the whistling factory children, hands feeling the smooth round coins in his pockets as he strode along like he was one of them.

Perfect. Ninepence! He had nearly a whole shilling for a few minutes' work. It was more than enough to feed him. Perhaps he'd lay low for the rest of the day—or then again, perhaps not.

He could hide out for a few minutes, then return to dip into the ever-flowing crowd that poured down this street like a river. Then he might have hot beef stew for dinner tonight instead of fish, apples, and cheese.

The bakery's smell made his mouth water. Or he could have a whole sticky bun all to himself. Or—

A watch chain gleamed in the corner of his eye. Jack drifted away from the crowd of children almost automatically. A gold watch, he realized. It had to be worth a fortune.

Jack didn't think twice. He slipped his hand into the bewhiskered old gentleman's pocket and whisked the gold watch into his own almost without thinking. Would the pawnbroker take a gold watch? He'd never minded taking stolen things before. He might get plenty of money for this. *Pounds instead of pennies.*

"Thief!" A piercing whistle and the clanging of a bell split the street's quiet bustle. "Stop, thief!"

The words energized the crowd. They jumped and looked around, clutching their bags, grabbing their pockets, and the bewhiskered old gentleman cried out in dismay.

"There, there!" a man cried. "There's the little thief!"

The crowd parted on Jack's left, and a uniformed bobby ran towards him, silver gleaming on his tall hat, truncheon swinging from his belt.

Jack cried out and spun around, the gold watch tumbling from his pocket as he did so.

"There!" the bewhiskered old gentleman yelled, striking out with his cane. It rang over Jack's shins, tripping him. Before he could fall to the ground, the bobby was upon him. His white-gloved hand closed on Jack's arm and yanked him back in an unbreakable grip.

"No!" Jack cried. "Please! Please! Let go!"

"My watch!" The old gentleman grabbed it. "It was a gift from my wife. Oh, you wretched little swine!" He brandished his cane.

"There's no need for that, sir." The bobby shook Jack so hard his teeth rattled. "This little scoundrel will hang! I saw him steal from you with my very eyes."

Hang. The word ripped through Jack's mind, and he remembered a time when he'd passed by some gallows with Smudge and the others. The man on the gallows had been red and boated when his legs stopped twitching.

"*NO!*" Jack screamed.

"Stop that, you little thief," the bobby snarled. "You've only yourself to blame for—"

An apple bounced off the back of the bobby's head. He jumped, his grip wobbling on Jack's arm. "Hey! Who did that?"

Jack cried out and writhed, almost too afraid to see that a small pebble bounced off the bobby's cheek a moment later. Irate, he looked around. "Who's throwing things?" he roared. "I am an office of the law!"

A rotten tomato struck him next. It splattered on his nose, sticky and reeking, and the bobby gave a wordless cry. His grip slackened for an instant. It was long enough. Jack twisted, his arm slipping through the bobby's grip, and bolted.

"Stop him!" the bobby roared.

Then Jack saw it: a cloud of red hair. Liz hurled a rotted apple with all her strength. It punched into the back of the bobby's head, and he whirled around, roaring. Jack swerved hard to avoid Liz, barely realizing how ridiculous her actions were, and sprinted away.

His heart hammered. His legs pistoned madly as he bolted through the crowd, but the cries of pursuit grew distant and faded to nothing as he reached his warehouse's door.

He lunged to yank it open, but before he could, a pale hand grabbed the doorknob and slammed it shut.

"You're not going anywhere," Finn growled.

Jack yelped and stumbled back, wildly looking around. The crowd on the street hurried past as always; no one looked at him except the tall blond boy with venom in his eyes.

Finn rubbed his hands. "Where do you think you're going?"

Jack turned to flee and almost ran headlong into Liz. She was eating an apple—only slightly wrinkled, this time—and her glittering eyes froze him to the spot.

"You're not running anywhere, kid," she said.

More children appeared out of nowhere. They surrounded Jack like something from a nightmare with their grimy faces and ragged clothes, all smiling and sneering, exposing missing and rotten teeth.

"Please," Jack whimpered. "Please, I'm sorry. Don't hurt me."

"We're not here to hurt you, boy," said Liz. She chewed the last of her apple's core. "If we were, we'd have hurt you already."

Jack eyed the door, but Finn stepped forward again, blocking his escape. There was nowhere to run.

"You're terrible at listening," said Liz. "Do you know that?"

"I'm sorry," Jack whimpered.

"No, you're not. If you were sorry, you'd have run away when I told you to. But I see you're not good at doing as you're told." Liz folded her arms. "You *are* good at stealing, though."

"Not that good," Finn muttered.

"Finn, enough," Liz snapped.

Finn pressed his lips together, but stayed silent.

"Please," Jack whispered. "Please let me go."

"Don't be so lily-livered, boy. Stand up straight," Liz ordered. "You weren't scared of me the first time, when you should have been, but you don't have to be scared of me now. Why do you think we distracted that bobby so you could get away?"

The rotten fruit. Jack blinked. "You... you did that?"

"Of course," said Liz. "Who else?"

"Why?" said Jack.

Liz grinned. "Like I said, boy, you're good at stealing." She shrugged. "So are we. We like that."

Finn growled, but said nothing.

"So, I want you to join our little crew," said Liz.

Jack stared at the children. "Crew?"

"It's safer out there when we stay together. We've got a good place to sleep. We split everything we make; everybody eats," said Liz. "What do you say?"

Jack stared at her. Suddenly, for no reason he knew, his mother flitted through his mind. He saw her smiling and laughing, saw her bouncing him on her knee. He heard her telling him, *Good boy, Jack-Jack. You're such a good boy.*

If he joined this gang, did that make him a good boy?

"We sleep warm with full bellies every night," one of the smaller children piped up. "It's real good."

Warm and full bellies. Jack thought of how nearly he'd been dragged away by the bobby that day, how he couldn't have made it without these other children.

"All right," he said. "I'll join."

Liz grinned as Finn looked away. "Good! What do we call you?"

"Jack," he said.

"Welcome, Jack." Liz slapped him on the back.

A small child with a tousle of black curls hugged his legs. "Welcome, Jack!"

The other children closed around him, wringing his hand and slapping his back. All except Finn. The big blond boy stayed to one side, arms folded, and sneered.

The old tenement building had long since been condemned, but if anyone still knew that, they'd clearly forgotten. Half of the roof was completely missing; the front of the building always squelched with mud. But here, in the back half, the children had fashioned something like a cosy home for themselves. Slats of metal and slabs of wood had been carried down from the upper stories to form a wall that made the roof feel solid. Boarded-up windows provided just enough space for the smoke to escape, and the dry, clean floor felt like a luxury.

Jack stretched out on a straw mattress—a real mattress! Before coming here, he had seen no such thing since Charlie's house—and interlaced his fingers behind his head.

He gazed contentedly at the ceiling as he relished the thought of dinner. Already, a cup of hot tea nursed his belly, and quiet conversation filled the warehouse as they waited for Liz, Millie, and Em to get back with supper.

Children drowsed on mattresses or thick piles of blankets and newspapers. A fire crackled in the centre of the floor, and the smoke vanished through the cracks in the much-mended ceiling.

Jack edged a little nearer to the flames and pillowed his head on his hands, delighting in the warmth and the knowledge that supper would come soon.

The happy thought became reality a few moments later as footsteps sounded across the floor and someone knocked on the door, a distinctive rhythm. The children jumped up as Finn moved the barrel that blocked the door aside and allowed in Liz with two of the smaller girls. They wore expressions of triumph, and a wonderful smell rolled into the room with them: something rich and buttery and spicy.

"Oh, Liz!" cried Ronnie, one of the smaller boys. "What do you have?"

"I said I'd bring you supper, didn't I?" Liz strode to the spool that served as a table near the fire, her face filled with triumph. "Tonight, we eat pie!"

She stacked four pie dishes on the table, their crusts golden in the firelight. The children gathered around, clamouring and laughing.

The pie crusts steamed; they were as fresh as could be.

"Baker put them on the windowsill to cool." Liz laughed. "Millie, Em and I snatched them before he knew what was coming to him."

"Pie!" Jack gasped, running over with the other children. He didn't think he'd ever tasted it, but the smell was breathtaking.

"Apple pie, Jackie boy," said Liz, "and you've earned it after the breakfast you stole for us." Jack had swiped a tray of sticky buns that morning.

"I brought bread for lunch," Finn mumbled, but nobody seemed to hear him.

"Come on, dig in," said Liz. "Divide up in groups of three, that's it. Here, Finn, you take this one. Joe, take this one." She picked up the third pie dish and glanced around, then focused on Jack. "Jack, here, you sit over there with Em and Ronnie."

"Yes, Liz." Jack gripped the warm dish and led the other children to a spot by the fire. They sat down on either side of them, and together, they dug into the dish with their fingers. There were no rules here, Jack had learned; one ate however one wanted. His workhouse matron would have caned him for eating like this, but now he didn't care. He shovelled a handful of hot pie from the tin and gulped it down.

"Mmm." Millie groaned with pleasure.

"Oh, that's wonderful," said Jack with his mouth full. The sweet, buttery, spicy flavours were breathtaking. "I've never eaten anything like that before."

"Didn't your mama ever make you pie?" Ronnie asked.

"Not everyone had a mama, Ronnie," said Liz bitterly.

"I didn't," said Millie. "I was always in the workhouse."

"Me too," said Em, "until I ran away."

"I had a papa, but he died," said Joe quietly.

"How about you, Jack?" Liz asked. "Did you have a mama?"

Jack smiled. "I have the best mama in the world," he said. "She's very, very beautiful and always kind. She has soft hands and loves me so very much. I know she'll find me again someday."

"Ha!" Finn snorted. "Everyone thinks that at first, but they never do."

"Wh-what do you mean?" Jack asked.

Finn glared at Jack with baleful, pale green eyes. "They never come back for us. Forget your mama, Jack. She doesn't care about you."

Tears filled Jack's eyes. "That's not true. It wasn't her fault that we're not together anymore."

"Tell yourself that, stupid," Finn growled.

"What does it matter?" Liz's voice broke through their argument. "We don't need mamas or papas, do we?" She smiled, apple pie staining her lips. "Who needs grownups at all when you have this? We're all the family any of us ever needs."

She gestured at the clutch of children sitting around the fire, their faces dirty, but their bellies full.

"That's right," said Finn.

Jack didn't agree, but he was glad for the pie, glad for the company, and glad for the sound of quiet breathing and tiny snores around him as he slowly dropped off to sleep later. It reminded him of being back among the soot sacks at Smudge's house.

He wondered if Beryl had a full belly tonight.

The thought ran him through like a lance.

Part Three

Chapter Six

Four Years Later

The crowd was always thick at this time on a Sunday morning. Everyone flowed from the churches in their Sunday best, flashing their gold pocket watches, their pockets full of money left over from collections. It was the best time of day for pickpocketing. Everyone knew that.

Jack leaned against a streetlamp, eating an apple left over from yesterday's work, and watched as the crowd flowed from the local church at the end of the street. It was high summer, with rare, bright sunshine flowing onto the street, and all of the ladies had pretty ribbons in their hair. The men wore flowers in their buttonholes and brighter, happier faces than before they entered the church.

Jack didn't know what it was inside the church that made them happy, but he knew what would make *him* happy very shortly.

He glanced across the street at the other children lurking in the shadows. Millie, who was enchanting with her big soft eyes, sang on a street corner. She'd make a few pennies, but she mostly served as a distraction. Finn leaned against a closed shop doorway. Joe and Em were hidden nearby, too; Liz and the others were down the street, running another trick.

In seconds, Jack spotted the perfect mark. A beautiful young woman with a head of thick dark hair, her laughter echoing down the street, jewellery sparkling at her neck and ears. A gold locket bounced on her chest as she ran after a well-dressed little toddler with polished shoes. She carried a baby on her hip, and an older child followed her.

She was rich, innocent, and had her hands full. She was perfect.

Jack nodded toward the woman and met Finn's eyes. Across the street, Finn frowned and shook his head. He inclined his head toward another mark—an older gentleman bent on berating his young son.

Angry people were more defensive. Jack shook his head again and moved on the young mother.

He slipped through the crowd, quick and easy, aware of Millie a few yards away on his left.

She suddenly changed her tune, clapping her hands as she sang, and the older child turned toward her.

"Look, Mama!" the child called. "She's singing!"

The toddler writhed from the mother's grasp. Baby bouncing on her hip, she gasped and hurried to grab the back of the toddler's coat, bending low. Though Jack was as tall as she, this made it all the easier for him to reach out and open the clasp of her locket with a simple flick of his hand. He whisked it into his pocket and kept walking, then dived down an alley.

A shadow eclipsed the alley mouth.

"What do you think you were doing?" Finn shouted.

Jack looked up and frowned. The big boy had his fists clenched, his cheeks tomato red beneath his pale hair. Though they were almost the same age, Finn towered over Jack, tall and lanky.

"Getting food to last us all day, and new blankets, too." Jack pulled out the locket and jingled it. "What does it look like?"

"Don't wave that around!" Finn barked. "Are you stupid?"

Em and Mille shuffled into the alley. "What's going on?" Em cried.

"Shut up, Em," Finn barked.

"Don't talk to her like that," said Jack.

"You can't tell me what to do!" Finn snapped.

"Neither can you," said Jack smartly. "I'm a leader like you now, remember? That's what Liz said."

Finn's cheeks flushed deeper scarlet, tendons standing out on his forearms as he clenched his fists. "You should never have gone for that mark."

"Why not? She was perfect," said Jack.

"Necklaces are a stupid thing to steal. What if she'd noticed?" Finn barked.

"She didn't. I'm too quick," said Jack.

"You didn't know that," Finn snapped.

Jack raised his chin, anger surging through him. "Maybe *you* can't steal necklaces, but I can."

Finn roared in anger.

"No!" Millie cried.

Em bolted as Finn lunged, swinging a fist toward Jack. He dodged, and the blow slammed into his shoulder instead. Shocked, Jack cried out and punched Finn in the belly.

The big boy doubled over, then slammed his shoulder into Jack and bore him to the ground.

Jack cried out as his back hit the ground. He squirmed, stronger though smaller than Finn, and shoved his knee hard into the other boy's leg. When Finn rolled over, Jack jumped on top. Finn roared with anger as Jack swung a wild punch that connected Finn's chest.

"Stop!" Millie cried. "Stop!"

Finn punched, the blow landing on Jack's jaw. Jack cried out in anger and seized two fistfuls of Finn's hair, feeling the blond strands rip from the bigger boy's scalp. Snorting like an angered warhorse, Finn squirmed beneath Jack and tried to hit him again.

"*Stop!*" Liz bellowed.

Her authoritative voice tore through the alley. Jack had released Finn's hair even before she grabbed him by the arm and hauled him to his feet. She shoved him aside, pulled Finn upright, and slammed him into the alley wall with one hand.

"Liz, he was—" Jack began.

Liz struck out with her other hand and pinned Jack into the opposite wall. She was breathing hard, her hair falling over her face, and pure rage burned in her eyes.

"What are you two louts thinking?" she bellowed. "Fools!"

"He started it!" Jack cried.

"I started it? You insulted me!" Finn roared.

"Stop it! Now!" Liz thundered.

They both fell silent, breathing hard, sweat and dirt smeared on their faces.

"We are a family," Liz snapped. "We don't behave like this. You frightened the life out of poor Em and Millie, and I heard you two idiots shouting all the way down the street. What if the bobbies had heard you and come running? What then, you fools?"

Jack hung his head.

"He's a hothead, Liz," Finn snapped. "He's a danger to the whole gang. We'd be better off without him. You should throw him out!"

Liz's head snapped around toward Finn, danger burning in her eyes. "You're lucky I don't throw *you* out," she hissed.

Finn blanched.

"Now behave, at once," Liz ordered, "or you'll both be sorry."

"Yes, Liz," they mumbled.

"In fact," said Liz, "tomorrow, you'll go and rob the grocer tomorrow. Together."

Finn and Jack stared at each other.

"You want us to work together?" Jack cried.

"I do. Things have gotten worse and worse between you two for the past year. Now you'll have no choice but to sort it out," Liz snapped. "You'd better not disappoint me."

Liz released them both and stormed away, taking Em and Millie with her. Finn stepped nearer to Jack, his size suddenly intimidating. Jack's chin and shoulder ached where Finn had struck him.

"This isn't over, you worm," Finn hissed in his face. He spat on Jack's feet.

"Finn!" Liz snapped.

The big boy turned and stormed off. Jack followed, heart pounding.

A thin, drizzly rain fell on the street as Jack and Finn plodded down the sidewalk toward the grocer's. The crowd was muffled and anonymous between their umbrellas and scarves as they hustled to and fro, splashing in puddles.

"I'll be the lookout," Jack muttered, breaking the icy silence that had hovered between them since leaving home that morning.

Finn shot him a vicious glare. "No. You'll go inside. We want a sack of apples. Can you remember that?"

Jack snorted. "Of course I can. Why should you be the lookout?" He didn't trust Finn to watch his back.

Finn sneered. "I thought you were the one with quick hands."

Jack's stomach clenched. He had no answer to that.

The icy silence returned as they approached the greengrocer's. With the rich summer upon them, the shelves were filled with colour: bright green apples, yellow lemons, pears in rich hues of red and gold, orange carrots, the deep green of chard and cabbage. Jack glanced over the produce as though casually. A few housewives were inside, feeling the fruit and vegetables, picking the juiciest ones to bring home to their families.

Finn took his position on the street corner. "Make it quick," he snarled.

Jack looked up and down the street, heart fluttering. He saw no bobbies, but that didn't mean they weren't there. What would Finn do if one of them appeared and grabbed him?

"Are you going in or not?" Finn demanded. "Don't be a coward."

"I'm no coward," Jack hissed.

He turned on his heel and stalked toward the greengrocer's, eyes fixed straight ahead as though he planned to pass by. Behind the counter, the elderly man nodded and smiled at the housewives. There was no threat in him; he'd lost a leg at sea, and hobbled around with a crutch. He couldn't chase thieves even if he tried.

Jack spotted the sacks of apples near the door and clenched his belly. This theft held no finesse. It was pure speed.

His feet moved fast. He darted through the door, saw the greengrocer's face twist in fury, and dived for the apple barrels. A lady sprang aside with a scream of terror as Jack's fingers closed around the rough burlap.

"Thief!" one lady cried. "Stop!"

A door thudded behind the counter. Jack didn't wait to see who came through it. He whirled around and bolted, and as he rushed through the door with the sack in his hands, he heard it: the most terrifying sound for any young thief.

The baying of a big dog.

Jack bolted through the door, slipped as he came out, and almost fell. As he scrambled to his feet, he glimpsed it: a huge brown mastiff, claws scrabbling on the wooden floor as it lunged from behind the counter, froth flying from its mouth.

"Finn!" Jack screamed, bolting. "Finn, dog! Dog!"

Finn jumped. He broke into a run as Jack reached him, and they sprinted into the street side by side as screams and cries resounded around them. The dog bayed again, and Jack instinctively dove into the crowded street.

Horses snorted, wheels screeched, and drivers cursed as Jack and Finn darted through the traffic. The apples bounced in the sack Jack clutched; he hung on for dear life as he darted past a brewer's dray and narrowly missed a lady on horseback. Her horse reared as the dog pursued them. Jack glanced back as the mastiff darted around it, jumped inches away from a carriage's wheels, and followed him and Finn onto the pavement.

"Alley!" Jack barked.

Finn swerved hard to the left. The alley was narrow, but it ended in a wall they could scale and the dog might not. Jack's heart thudded in his mouth as he grabbed a streetlamp to swivel himself after Finn. An apple flew from his sack and bounced away; he felt the loss but kept running.

Puddles gleamed in the alley between piles of nameless debris. Finn sprinted toward the shoulder-high wall at the end. A rotting barrel lying to one side provided a springboard, and Finn's long legs stretched toward it.

Jack didn't see the discarded tin until Finn stepped on it. The tin rolled beneath the bigger boy's grimy shoe, and Jack saw his ankle twist inward before Finn collapsed to the ground with a scream of pain.

"Finn!" Jack cried.

He skidded to a halt over Finn, who lay sobbing in the mud, and looked up. He couldn't see the mastiff yet, but its baying was close—very close.

Finn clutched his ankle, weeping with pain. He would never be able to climb that wall. But Jack could. One quick leap and he'd be over the wall and safe... leaving Finn to his face, just as he'd left Beryl.

Jackie! Her scream reverberated through his mind, as painfully clear as it had done on the night he'd left her.

Finn's eyes snapped open as Jack's hands closed over his arm. He hauled the bigger boy to a sitting position.

"Come on!" Jack cried. "Quickly!"

Finn scrambled upright, heavily leaning on Jack. A few yards away, a rubbish bin lay on its side, rotting food spilling from it. Jack half dragged Finn toward it as the mastiff's roars grew nearer. He lifted it upright and they stuffed their skinny bodies inside, pulling the lid shut over themselves as the dog's paws scrabbled around the turn into the alley.

Finn was sobbing with pain, his lanky body squished against Jack in the tight, smelly space. Filth squelched beneath their feet.

"Shhh," Jack whispered. "Shhh."

Finn held his breath. Jack tried to take small breaths, fighting the urge to gag on the terrible stench.

The dog's snarling stopped. They heard its collar jingle as it ran into the alley. It sniffed loudly, growing nearer and nearer. Jack feared it would hear the wild thundering of his heart.

Then, distantly, a voice called. The dog gave a joyous bark and bounded away.

"I think he's gone," Finn whispered.

Jack pushed the lid off the rubbish bin and scrambled out. He helped Finn, who hopped on one leg, his face twisted with pain. Slowly and painstakingly, they scrambled over the wall, Finn leaning heavily on Jack as they eased down to the other side.

The apples were long gone. Jack couldn't worry about them now; Liz and the others would make sure that there was food today. All he needed to do was get Finn safely home.

The bigger boy leaned on him, unable to put weight on his wounded foot, as they slowly hopped down the other side of the alley. They'd nearly reached the street when Finn said, "You came back."

Jack said nothing.

"I've been awful to you," said Finn, "but you came back."

There was a long pause. Jack didn't know what to say, and Finn said nothing more about it. But in that moment, everything changed.

CHAPTER SEVEN

Sticky sugar ran over Jack's chin, making him forget the cruel nip of autumn in the air. He giggled as he caught the dripping sugar with a finger and thrust his finger in his mouth to suck down the incredible sweetness. The sticky bun in his other hand clung to his fingers, its soft doughy innards tearing apart.

"The new baker is wonderful," Finn groaned.

"Yes! We'll be back," Jack agreed.

"We shouldn't steal from him," Finn decided. "Or he might not sell things to us anymore."

"I agree." Jack sucked his fingers, then bit into the sticky bun again. They'd spent a pleasant morning picking pockets for the money for their sweet, delicious breakfast. Finn carried a paper bag with buns for the other children, too.

"Em's going to be so happy." Finn chuckled. "There's nothing she loves more than a sticky bun."

"We should get a whole bag for everyone at Guy Fawkes Day," said Jack.

"Guy Fawkes Day is weeks away." Finn laughed.

Jack grinned. "It's never too early to think about it." The rich folk of their area always built an effigy in the middle of the market square and set it alight while people danced and laughed. Jack didn't know why they did so, but the distracted crowd made for easy pickings.

"How's your ankle after all that running?" Jack asked, sucking the last sugar off his fingers.

Finn shrugged. "It's all right."

"Good." Jack grinned. "Isn't it wonderful how Liz talked that apothecary into selling her the medicine for the pain?"

"Liz can get anything we need," said Finn.

It was true. They never slept cold or hungry, not with Liz looking out for them, and the children all looking out for each other. Despite the grey clouds gathering overhead, threatening rain,

Jack felt no fear the way he used to do before he joined Liz's crew. They'd spend the afternoon sprawled around the fire, talking and dozing while rain drummed on the roof.

"One more bun," said Finn. "We'll share it." He retrieved it from the paper bag and tore it in half.

"One more," Jack agreed.

He took his half and bit into it, humming. Contentment spread through him—a feeling unlike anything he'd known since losing Mama. These children were his family, he knew. He could be happy like this forever.

They reached the street's end, and Finn turned left, munching his bun. Jack stopped dead.

"Do we have to go this way?" he asked.

"C'mon, Jack," said Finn easily. "The workhouse won't bite you. It's much quicker."

Jack bit his lip. "You know I don't like to go past there."

"Not even to get Em her sticky buns faster?" Finn tantalizingly shook the bag.

Jack tasted rich sugar on his tongue and sighed. "Oh, all right. I suppose you're right."

They set off once more, and Jack nonetheless felt a knot in his belly as the tall brick building loomed ahead. Tall iron palisades enclosed the heartless yards surrounding the workhouse, yards where he'd once gone out for exercise with other tiny boys. He didn't recall much of those days, but he remembered everything being bare and grey and lonely. He remembered the older boys' fists.

"Don't look at it," said Finn. "Think about something else. Here, have another bun."

Jack had lost his appetite, but his friend's voice reminded him that the workhouse was no longer his reality. He was no longer one of those poor little children sitting around in the exercise yards, their eyes empty, wearing ugly black and white stripes. They watched with hollow eyes as Jack licked the last sugar from his fingers.

"Poor wretches," said Finn. "I'm glad we're not in there."

"Me too," said Jack fervently, and then he saw her.

She sat with her side to him, legs folded underneath her, leaning against the wall and staring at nothing. A smaller girl lay with her head in her lap, and her delicate little fingers played with the little girl's hair. Jack stopped dead. Surely he was wrong. It had been six years...

And yet nothing could make him forget that particular tilt of her nose, the rich colour of her hair. No one had hair like that, so red, so bushy, so vivid.

Jack distantly heard Finn saying his name. He stood rooted to the spot, gaping at her.

It couldn't be. Surely not.

Then another girl called across the yard. "Beryl!"

She raised her head, red curls spilling over her shoulders. The little girl in her lap sat up, and Beryl rose and crossed the yard in small, defeated steps, her little shoulders hunched.

Jackie!

He heard her scream, and the memory sliced through him, reminding him of all the ways in which he'd failed. He remembered screaming the words at her. *I hate you! I hate you!*

He'd meant it, in that moment, but now he wondered if those words had anything to do with her slumping shoulders and hanging head. Did they play over and over in her mind as they did in his?

"Jack!" Finn shook him. "What is it?"

The little girls filed back into the workhouse. Jack turned away.

"You look like you've seen a ghost," said Finn.

Jack had seen a ghost: the haunting of what he'd done. It followed him all the way back to the tenement and into his dreams that night.

I'm so sorry, Jackie. I'm so sorry. I'm so sorry!

Beryl's panicked cry and tear-streaked face filled Jack's mind. He could still hear himself screaming those hateful words at her, those words he'd meant in the moment despite the fact that she was the closest thing he had to family.

I'm so sorry!

Jack rubbed his face, trying to make the memory leave, and forced his attention back to the street. It was late afternoon on a Thursday, and a hasty crowd filled the sidewalks and dodged the carriages rattling by, desperate to get home before the storm broke. The slate-grey sky ominously rumbled above.

He wasn't worried about the busy street. He scanned it again, looking for the tell-tale shape of a bobby's hat or the flash of a black and silver uniform. Seeing nothing, Jack exhaled and rubbed his hands, relieved his wandering mind hadn't endangered the others.

He dared not glance back at the sweatshop behind him. Millie had hopelessly outgrown her clothes thanks to the far richer fare they'd had for the past few weeks now that Jack and Finn worked together. They ate three times a day these days, and a huge variety: soup, bread, apples, cheese, fish, chicken, and vegetables. Even sweetmeats, quite often.

And how did Beryl eat? Did she survived as Jack did when he was a tiny boy in the workhouse, on gruel and bread, on scraps left over once the bullies had had their share?

His gut clenched. The overwhelming feeling that he shouldn't be here once again washed over him. He had stolen bread the night he'd left Smudge's. He'd stolen the night he broke Beryl's heart.

Now here he was, having learned nothing, stealing again. What would she think of him? How would she see him, this luxurious scoundrel, who lay on warm blankets and ate apple pie he'd snatched from a shop window?

"No! Stop!" The scream came from the sweatshop. "Thieves! Thieves!"

Jack blinked, snapping back to the present, and the sound they all feared more than anything tore through the air. The shrill whistle of a policeman.

"By Jove!" Liz cried as she scrambled through the sweatshop door, arms full of stolen goods. "There's a bobby right over there!"

The bobby burst through the crowd, truncheon swinging, mere yards away.

"Run!" Jack screamed.

"Now you tell us!" Liz roared.

She darted into the crowd, Em and Joe close behind her. Jack stared at the charging bobby, open-mouthed and horrified.

A hand closed on his arm. "Come on!" Finn roared, yanking Jack after him.

They broke into a run and bolted down the street. The thick crowd cried out in exasperation; Jack made sure to brush against several of them and anger them. Then they spun around, stepping right into the bobby's path. For a few heart-wrenching moments, it seemed that the plan wasn't working. Then Jack and Finn followed Liz and the others down the alley and over the ever-handy wall, and the bobby's whistles faded into the distance.

Liz slowed from a run to a jog, then a walk. When she turned to Jack, her eyes were like twin green flames. She raised a hand and cuffed him on the back of the head. It wasn't a hard blow, but it shocked him so much that he stumbled to a halt.

"What were you doing out there, Jackie?" she demanded.

"Um... I didn't see him," Jack croaked.

"Didn't see him?" Liz threw her arms in the air. "He was right on top of us! Do you know what could have happened if he'd caught us?"

Em and Joe stared up at Jack with round eyes, leaving him painfully aware of the truth.

"I know," he mumbled. "I'm sorry."

"You haven't been yourself for days," Liz snapped. "You need to sort yourself out or we're all in trouble, Jack. You can't do this to us. We rely on you."

The words landed like a knife in Jack's belly. Beryl had relied on him, too, and look at what he'd done to her.

"I'm sorry," he mumbled.

"Yes, you'd better be," Liz snapped. She turned on her heel and strode away, the other children staying close to her.

Jack hung his head and followed more slowly. Finn matched pace with him and laid a hand on his shoulder.

"What's wrong, Jack?" he asked. "You haven't been the same since we went past that workhouse. I wish you'd tell me what you saw there."

Tears filled Jack's eyes. He fought them back with difficulty. He'd never told Finn, or anyone, about Beryl; he was far too ashamed about what he'd done to her.

"Please, Jackie," said Finn.

Jack swallowed hard. "Do you... do you ever think about what we're doing?" he murmured.

Finn frowned. "What do you mean?"

"Well, does it seem right to you?" Jack asked.

Finn blinked. "Of course it does. We're hungry. We need food. What's to think about?"

"But we're stealing," said Joe. "We're taking things from people."

Finn scoffed. "Lockets from rich women who don't care that we're starving."

"All the same..." Jack shook his head. "There are other ways. You've heard how they cry when we take their things.

And the shop owners… Remember that bakery that went out of business after we'd cleared it out?"

Finn grinned. "We ate well that night."

"Yes, but…" Jack shook his head. "It doesn't seem right, Finn. What we're doing is wrong. I know it."

Finn slapped Jack on the back. "Come on, Jackie. That's just silly. Look how good our lives are! Surely nothing that makes us this happy could be wrong."

"I know, but—" Jack began.

"Oh, stop fussing," said Finn. "Come on. I can't wait to see Millie in her new clothes, can you?"

Jack mustered a smile for Finn's sake. But it still felt as though their actions shackled his heart.

The church bell struck eight as Jack jogged along the street. The other children in the gang would barely stir until nine; they'd feasted on stolen fish and chips, snatched from a vendor's cart, and had no need of breakfast. They'd played and danced well into the night.

Except for Jack. He'd slept fitfully, his dreams haunted by the fish vendor's cries of dismay.

Now, he slunk toward the workhouse. The morning light cast the palisades' shadows like bars across the street, ready to trap Jack within. He stayed near the stone pillars that housed the palisades, trying to avoid the angry eyes of the workhouse staff. From his experience, they were always, always angry.

Jack peered around the pillar and into the yard where he'd seen Beryl weeks before. Its bare stone floor offered no comfort; the sheer brick walls on three sides held no decoration. Only the bars nearest Jack offered any view, and that was only a strip of bare street and the immovable wall of a tenement building. This was Beryl's entire world, apart from a smelly dining hall and a dormitory filled with lice. Jack knew; he'd been here.

The little girls filed out of the workhouse with hanging heads and limp arms. How different they were to Liz's gang, who bounded from their abandoned building laughing and pushing one another. Then again, Jack remembered the hunger that weighed on his limbs when he was in the workhouse. He, too, had lifelessly shuffled from the cold building into the colder day.

Beryl was in the middle of the line. She had her arms wrapped around her body, shivering in the chill wind; her striped dress offered her little protection. Jack felt the rising urge to strip off his jacket and give it to her. But the matron would punish her, for one thing.

She'd see him, for another, and Jack didn't think he could bear that.

The children fanned out. One or two little girls skipped half-heartedly; the rest gathered in a miserable huddle in the only corner of the yard that held any sunlight. Beryl slid down with her back against the wall and sat there with her eyes closed, hands folded in her lap. Her red hair seemed dull in the sunshine.

Tears rolled in warm silence down Jack's cheeks. He longed to extend a hand to her, to grasp her arm and whisk her away. It was a wild, foolish thought, but he found his hand rising toward her after all, longing to give her a better life.

Then, suddenly, she turned her head.

Her eyes found his. They were unchanged: the brightest, clearest, gem-like blue. Her lips parted. Jack instantly saw recognition on her face.

Beryl knew him. She knew he was the one who'd left her, who'd broken her heart. He wished to see anger in her eyes, but instead, he saw something far worse: wild hope.

She hoped he was here to help her. She hoped he was something more than a thief, a liar, and a traitor who'd abandoned her.

He couldn't bear for her to see what he'd become. Jack whirled around and bolted into the streets, his tears flowing faster than ever.

Chapter Eight

Jack gazed longingly to the left as the knot of children approached the crossroads. The sweatshop robbery a few weeks ago had been followed by a few others; everyone now wore warm coats, hats, and mittens, bundled against the nippy cold. The low, grey sky promised rain later.

That meant that the workhouse children wouldn't go out to the exercise yards today. Jack's only chance to glimpse Beryl today was rapidly slipping through his fingers, and over the past few weeks, Sundays had become his favourite day to see her. He could watch her walking over to the chapel in the corner of the workhouse. She'd pass so close to the palisades, close enough for him to see the redness of her eyes, but the matron was strict and ensured that the children kept their gazes forward. She wouldn't see him.

And now he was missing it.

Finn elbowed Jack in the ribs. He jumped.

"Jack, for the last time," Liz snapped, "are you paying attention?"

"Yes, Liz," Jack lied. He was a thief, after all. Why not a liar, too? Still, his guts knotted at the thought.

Liz's eyes narrowed. "Then you'll know what you have to do. Get your head out of the clouds, Jack."

"Or out of the workhouse," Millie chipped in. The other children giggled.

"Go on. Finn, make sure Jack stays focused," Liz ordered.

They split up as they approached the church down the road from the workhouse. In contrast to the workhouse's stark appearance, the church was beautifully decorated, with whitewashed walls and pretty gardens, the trees' branches bare against the grey sky. Liz, Em, Millie, and Joe wriggled into the hole in the hedge and waited there. Jack and Finn loitered on the corner, kicking a pebble back and forth, pretending to be totally disinterested as the first few carriages approached the church. While some people came on foot, it was the carriages that interested Jack and Finn. They glanced up occasionally to watch as shining horses—which probably ate better than the children in the workhouse—halted in front of the church and handsome people disembarked from the carriages.

Poor Beryl, starved and alone. Jack couldn't bear to think of it.

"Jack, focus," Finn hissed.

Jack blinked. "Is that her?"

Finn swiftly glanced over his shoulder. "No. Her horses are both black."

Jack nodded and kicked the pebble back toward Finn, who returned it.

"You know you have to get this right," Finn whispered. "Or else Liz will be furious."

Silently, Jack nodded again.

A new carriage rattled down the street toward the church, this one drawn by two fine black horses with flowing manes.

"That's her," Jack hissed.

He and Finn dropped their pretence with the pebble and briskly moved across the street. They were halfway across when Em burst from the hedge right on time, the other children close beside her, waving sticks and shouting like maniacs.

The horses reared in panic. The driver yelled and hauled on the reins. *Fool*, Jack thought. He was making their terror worse, but it was good news for Liz's crew.

Jack and Finn darted around the carriage as the driver shouted, "Get out, m'lady, get out!" and the horse flew backwards, wood splintering in the shaft as they drove their haunches against the carriage.

The door crashed open. An old woman wailed in terror and jumped out, her extravagant jewellery jingling, and Jack and Finn were upon her before the helpful crowds could reach her. She slipped as her feet met the sidewalk and landed hard on her hands and knees with a cry of pain.

Jack froze.

"Come on!" Finn roared, already crouching beside the old woman. She screamed in terror as he seized her handful of necklaces and yanked them over her head, then pulled a pearl-encrusted comb from her hair.

"Jack, move it!" Liz thundered.

Her voice startled Jack into action. He dived forward, grabbing the purse that fell from the old woman's hands, and then the pastor was rushing from the church.

"Emma!" he cried.

"Run, run!" Liz yelled.

Finn jumped clean over the old lady and bolted into the crowd. Jack swerved, avoiding the calming horses, and sprinted in the other direction as planned. A few half-hearted pursuers started after him, but none could be bothered to dirty their Sunday best. When Jack skirted sideways down a narrow, soot-streaked alley and scaled a wall into a nearby manure heap, they left him alone.

He jogged to a halt on the other side, breathless, and walked quietly toward the tenement building. The old lady's purse jingled in his pocket, filled with the promise of all the clothes and food and sweetmeats and blankets he could dream of.

Yet he felt as though he was carrying a purse full of filth with him.

He reunited with the other children on the street corner, and their joy shocked him. Finn was grinning and elated as he pounded little Joe on the back.

"You scared the life out of those horses!" He chortled. "Well done, Joe!"

"It worked perfectly." Liz beamed. "Look at all this!" She raised the necklaces Finn had stolen; jewels and gold glinted in her hands.

"I think she was hurt," said Jack. "The old lady."

"She kicked Millie the other day when she was pretending to be a beggar, don't you remember?" Liz snorted. "She had it coming."

The other children led the way to the pawnshop, chuckling. Jack followed, head hanging, feeling deep in his belly that their actions that day had been cruel and evil.

Quiet breathing surrounded Jack. The fire burned in low, warm embers, its warmth filling the abandoned building.

So different from a workhouse dormitory, draughty and filled with sobbing children.

Jack cautiously lifted his head and looked around. None of the sleeping figures around the fire stirred. Silently, he rolled to his feet and got to work. He quietly rolled up two of the blankets on which he lay; he'd purchased them himself—albeit with money he'd stolen. Then he picked up the handful of coins Liz had given him after they'd pawned yesterday's loot. It was one-fifth of the total that was left over after the day's food. It was his.

He was done with stealing.

Jack slipped the coins into his pocket, tied the blankets with string, and tucked them under his arm. Then he tiptoed toward the slab of wood that served as a door. He didn't pause before lifting the wood aside; he knew that if he looked back, he wouldn't be able to leave.

After replacing the wood, Jack jogged across the creaky, starlit expanse toward the building's main door. He'd nearly reached it when a soft word floated across the space toward him.

"Jack."

Jack stopped. His heart sank, and he turned around slowly.

Finn stood amid the rubble behind him, his big hands hanging limp by his sides. The light of the streetlamp outside painted horror on the big boy's pale face.

"Where are you going?" Finn whispered.

Jack sighed. Hugging his blankets, he turned back. "I'm sorry, Finn. I… I can't do this anymore."

"Is this about the workhouse?" Finn asked. "You know they won't let you be near that girl you always watch if you go there."

"I'm not going to the workhouse," said Jack.

"Then where are you going?"

Jack looked away. "I'll buy a broom." He cleared his throat. "I'll be a crossing-sweeper."

"A sweeper?" Finn shook his head. "Why would you do that, Jack? You hardly earn anything and everyone treats you terribly."

"It's better than this," said Jack.

Finn stared at him.

"Don't you know that it's wrong to steal, Finn? My mama always said so when I was very little." Jack swallowed. "I've done so, so many bad and wrong and evil things in my life. Didn't you hear that poor old lady scream when she fell? What if she'd been killed? I can't do this."

"But you can leave us," said Finn. His voice was rough with tears. "You can leave me."

Jack stared up at him. "You could come, too. We could be sweeps together."

"And live where?" Finn asked. "Sleep where? On the streets?"

Jack said nothing.

"No... no." Finn backed away, shaking his head. "I can't do that again. Never again."

"Then I'm sorry, Finn." Jack turned away. "I... I hope you'll be safe. Please tell Liz and the others that I'm sorry. I just had to go. I'll miss all of you."

Finn made a tiny, strangled sound of pure sorrow. It wasn't a horrified scream like Beryl had given when Jack left her, but it still haunted him as he turned and left the tenement building for the last time.

The old man approaching the crossing seemed a likely sort. He held a little boy's hand—perhaps his grandson—and laughed at something the rotund and rosy child said as they waited for the traffic to clear. Jack tightened his grip on the broom handle, then instantly regretted it.

It seemed that pickpocketing gave one soft hands. He'd lost the strong calluses he'd once had as a chimney sweep; now, raw blisters had opened on Jack's palms in only a few days of working his new broom across the cobbles.

But he didn't have time for pain. If he was going to have any breakfast, he needed to charm this gentleman—and he longed for food. He'd only eaten a heel of bread the day before.

Jack jogged across the street and doffed his hat to the gentleman, smiling. "Top of the morning to you, sir!" He gripped the broom and worked swiftly, sweeping scraps of straw and road apples aside. The smell of horse manure filled the air, making the little boy's nose wrinkle, and Jack quickly swept it away even further.

"Where are we going now, Grandpapa?" the boy asked.

His grandfather smiled as they stepped off the curb and walked along the newly cleaned cobbles. "Well, my boy, how would you like cake for your dinner?"

"Cake!" The boy's eyes shone. "Can it be chocolate, Grandpapa?"

"It can be anything you like." The grandfather beamed, wrinkling his many chins.

Cake. Jack's stomach screamed at the word, but he could hear coins jingling in the old man's pockets. He would give him a penny or two, Jack was sure. He would have to.

He finished sweeping the crossing with a little flourish of his broom and a bow, then held out his cap to the grandfather. "Thank you kindly, sir," he said, "and have a lovely—"

The grandfather didn't so much as look at him. "We could even get two cakes," he said.

"Two cakes!" The little boy laughed.

The grandfather brushed against Jack's cap, almost knocking it out of his hand, and continued down the street without a glance back.

Jack slowly replaced his cap on his head. Thunder rolled overhead, and he shivered, thinking of the alley corner where he'd tucked away his blankets. The night before, they'd been soaked. He'd slept curled in the wet blankets as rain poured down on the roof of the cardboard shelter he'd made for himself.

Hopefully, he'd sleep dry tonight. Hopefully, he'd eat today.

Hopefully.

Jack's hope ebbed low. He swung his broom onto his shoulder and set off, head low, to remind himself why he could never go back to Liz's crew, no matter how cold or scared or hungry he was.

The walk to the workhouse was longer than before. Terrified of running into Liz, Jack had chosen a crossing on the other side of the block, one which the children seldom frequented thanks to the bobby who favoured the tea shop on the corner. Still, it was only a few minutes later that Jack rounded the corner and peered through the palisades.

It had rained for days. This would be the little girls' first time outside in almost a week, and for once, Jack heard laughter coming from the exercise yard. Many of the smaller girls ran around, giggling as they chased one another; even starved children felt the need to go outside and move around. Several older girls sat with their backs to the wall, arms folded, eyes closed as they tried to snatch a little sleep. But Beryl wasn't among them.

This time, she was with the little ones, running and playing. Her laugh filled Jack's world. Her red hair streamed over her shoulders, her skinny legs buckling with her feeble strides, but she was smiling. It was the first time he'd seen her smile in six long years. He'd forgotten how wide it was, how bright her blue eyes.

Jack leaned his head against the palisades and watched her. The sight made his hunger lessen, made the sun seem warmer.

When they were little, Beryl always looked at him like he was a hero.

He'd already proven a hundred times that he wasn't. But if he clung to the scrap of honest work he'd found, maybe he could start to make up for those times.

The little girl's chubby pink hands gripped the chair leg. Sitting on the kitchen floor, the flagstones warmed by the massive hearth, the baby furrowed her little brow into an expression of deep concentration.

Mabel stood by the kitchen table, kneading dough. Laughter came from outside, mingling with the deep tones of Percy's voice. It was the most perfect sound in the world, but now, Mabel's youngest baby captured her attention.

"Are you going to stand, darling?" Mabel asked. "Will you show Mama how nicely you stand?"

The baby giggled at her mother's voice. Her name was Margaret after Percy's mother, though she had yet to grow into it; for now, everyone knew her as Maggie.

She gripped the chair leg and hauled herself upright, wobbling on her stockinged feet. Her little bonnet bobbed as she stood.

"Clever girl, Maggie!" Mabel wiped her hands on a cloth and moved nearer. "Look at you, standing up!"

Maggie giggled toothlessly and released the chair. Hands high, she wobbled on her feet, her soft eyes locked on her mother's face.

"That's it!" Mabel crouched down and held out her hands. "Can you walk for Mama, sweetie? Can you?"

Maggie gave a fat, chortling laugh. Her rosy cheeks glowed beneath bright eyes as she extended her arms toward Mabel and took a wobbling, toddling step forward.

"That's it!" Mabel laughed. "That's it, darling! Look at you!"

Maggie toddled three more steps and collapsed into Mabel's arms. She straightened, swinging the child into a cradling hug, and showered kisses on the baby's soft pink cheeks.

Percy crashed through the door, bundled up in a thick coat, their three-year-old boy on his shoulders. Both had windblown hair and smelled of autumn leaves, which were stuck to their clothes.

"Percy!" Mabel cried. "Maggie walked!"

"She *walked*!" Percy gasped. "Did you hear that, Eddie?"

The little boy on his shoulders squealed with laughter. "I can walk, too."

"But this was Maggie's first time." Percy beamed. "Maggie can walk, Maggie can walk!" He danced around the room, bouncing Eddie on his shoulders.

Mabel laughed at their antics; in her arms, little Maggie joined in. It was a beautiful, perfect moment, and yet suddenly the old sorrow descended over her like a cold, wet towel on her shoulders. One moment she was laughing; the next she choked back tears.

Percy swiftly noticed, as he always did. He swung Eddie to the ground. "Hurry upstairs, Eddie boy," he said. "It's almost bath time."

The toddler ran out, giggling. Mabel had time to set Maggie gently on the hearth before her tears overflowed. She cried quietly—a mother had to—and Percy gently wrapped her in his arms.

"I'm sorry," Mabel whimpered.

"I know, darling." Percy kissed her hair. "I know."

"It's just—I remember it like it was yesterday," Mabel sobbed. "I remember Little Jack's first time walking. It was so beautiful, Percy. I didn't know anything then; I didn't know it was about to happen. It was like a miracle."

"Of course it was." Percy squeezed her.

Mabel stepped out of his arms and dried her eyes on her sleeves. "I wish he was here, too." She swallowed hard. "I miss him so, so much. I know it's been years, but..."

"You'll never stop missing him," said Percy gently. "I know that. I know how I'd feel if Maggie or Eddie were taken away from me." He squeezed her hands. "That's how you feel about Jack-Jack."

Mabel took deep breaths, soothing her tears away. "Have you heard anything new from the investigator?"

"I'm sorry, love." Percy shook his head. "Still nothing new. We'll visit him again when we go to London next week."

"Thank you." Mabel dried her face. "I hope... well... I hope he doesn't say... what he said last time."

Percy frowned. "Don't let that bother you, darling. It hasn't been too long, whatever he says. And if he tries anything like that again, he'll be fired, like the last one."

"How can there be so many quacks?" Mabel shook her head. "Don't they know how much they break my heart?"

"I'm sorry, darling." Percy put an arm around her shoulders and squeezed. "But I won't let him give up. None of us will ever give up on our Little Jack."

Mabel leaned her head against Percy's shoulder. *Oh Lord*, she prayed, *please, don't give up on him, either. Wherever he is, keep him safe. Let him find You. Let me find him.*

Part Four

Chapter Nine

Two Years Later

The boiled egg tasted better than the sweetest sticky bun. Jack forced himself to eat slowly, relishing every cold bite as he choked it down, then started on the wedge of slightly mouldy cheese.

He sat on a pile of newspapers in the doorway of a small, abandoned cottage. The door was locked fast, but nobody seemed to mind if he slept curled up on the doorstep. The newspapers had been a wonderful find; before buying them from a fellow street urchin, Jack used to sleep on the cold, bare stone.

The cheese filled his mouth. Its flavour had turned, but Jack could hardly care less. He choked it down and took another bite, and all too quickly, it was all gone.

Jack closed his eyes and leaned his head against the door.

It was so tempting to sit here today. He had eaten; it was a good day. But if he wanted to eat tomorrow, he didn't have a choice but to rise from the doorstep and plod toward the crossing.

It had changed in the two years since Jack had started sweeping it. More traffic had come here thanks to several new shops. At first, Jack had enjoyed having more customers. But then there came more crossing-sweepers. And they brought nothing but trouble with them.

He lurked beneath a street sign, feeling his strength return; the egg and cheese had been his first meal in two days. He turned the well-worn broom over in his callused hands, thinking that it was nearly time to replace the twigs that formed its brush. He could buy them from a starving little flower-seller who always struggled at this time of year.

A bright young voice floated through the air. Jack sighed as a little boy skipped across the street toward an aged woman who was about to cross.

"Lavender blue, dilly dilly," he sang, working his broom over the cobblestones. "Lavender green. When I am king, dilly dilly, you shall be queen."

The woman laughed. "Aren't you darling!"

The little boy sang gallantly as he swept the crossing, and though it took him a while, the old woman didn't seem to mind. She smiled and nodded her head along with the song; when they reached the other side, she handed the boy a sixpence.

Jack watched hungrily as the sixpence disappeared into the boy's pocket. He gritted his teeth and ordered himself to focus as another woman approached the crossing, this time a handsome middle-aged lady weighed down with shopping baskets. He strode toward her, smiling brightly as he doffed his cap.

"Lovely afternoon to you, m'lady!" he called, and got to work.

The woman barely glanced at him. He knew better than to try to sing; his voice had broken, and sounded awful. She strutted along as he swept the cobbles, repeatedly looking sideways at another lady crossing the street. Jack's stomach clenched in dismay.

The sweeper on that side of the street was a full-grown man, working the broom twice as fast as Jack could hope to do.

He shoved a small pile of manure aside and gave the woman a hopeful smile. She emitted a longsuffering sigh and produced a thruppence coin, which felt tiny and light in Jack's hand as he thanked her and closed his fingers over it.

The woman hurried off. Jack tucked the coin into his pocket and tried not to think of the last time he'd tasted a sticky bun, or of sleeping in warm blankets by a fire, or the sound of laughter, or playing with other children. He thrust those thoughts far away and raised his chin.

Then he looked up and down the street, searching for his next client.

"You should know, Mr. Goulding," said Mabel, "that you're the fourth investigator we've engaged on this matter. None of the others have done any good, and it's been ten years since I held my little boy."

Nathan Goulding blinked, startled by her boldness. The investigator sat behind a large, well-made mahogany desk. His office was on the top floor of a building not far from the courthouse Percy frequently visited, and Mabel tried to draw comfort from the deep carpet, the polished brass fittings on the gas lamps, and the newspaper clippings framed on the walls, all featuring cases this investigator had solved. *GOULDING DOES IT AGAIN!* one headline proclaimed.

"You come well recommended," Mabel added. "I only hope that you're willing to give this case the attention it deserves." She paused. "I'm willing to pay you well." Her farm had been doing better every year; she saved each spare penny for finding Jack.

"I'm sorry for your experience with other investigators, Mrs. Mitchell," said Nathan. He was a tall, craggy man with a striking, curly moustache, jet black against his alabaster skin. "Allow me to assure you that I haven't been taking your Jack's case lightly."

Mabel raised her head, startled that Nathan remembered Jack's name without having to consult his notes.

"Where is your husband today?" Nathan gently asked.

"He's still in court. It's running late, and I didn't want to miss our appointment." Mabel cleared her throat. "Rest assured that whatever you would say to him, you can say to me."

Nathan studied her for a moment. "Yes, I can see that." He spread his hands.

Mabel's stomach dropped. Was he going to tell her that her little boy was dead?

Or the same old story the other investigators had always given—that there was no way to find someone after so many years?

"I'm afraid my progress has been limited," said Nathan.

Mabel hung her head and squeezed her eyes shut against the disappointment. She'd sent this man pounds of her money, and all for the same result.

"I've only been able to find information on the chimney sweep who apprenticed Jack from the workhouse," Nathan went on.

Mabel's head snapped up. "You have?"

"Yes. It seems he gave the workhouse an alias, Reginald Grimshaw," said Nathan. He opened a neatly kept notebook on the desk. "I made enquiries among homeowners in the area.

Several have lived there for less than eight years, but those who've been there a while told me that they've met a sweep matching Grimshaw's description."

Mabel leaned forward, breathless. It was the first time she'd heard anything new about Jack in ten years.

"I won't bore you with the investigative details, Mrs. Mitchell. They're all in this report."

Nathan pushed it across the desk toward her. "I can tell all you want is to know what happened to Jack, and I'm sorry to say that I'm still not sure. But I can tell you this. The sweep who apprenticed Jack from the workhouse was Jeremiah Blackwood, who went by 'Smudge.' He had a small crew of sweep children with whom he worked in houses in the area."

"Was Jack one of them?" Mabel whispered.

"Yes." Nathan smiled. "I spoke to one house owner who remembered a little boy named Jack who was about the right age, but he was last seen eight years ago."

Eight years was less than ten. That meant that somebody had seen Jack as a six-year-old. Tears filled Mabel's eyes; thanks to long practice, she forced them back.

"Was he all right?" she asked.

Nathan hesitated.

"The truth, Mr. Goulding." Mabel swallowed her tears. "I want the truth."

"Yes, Mrs. Mitchell." Nathan sighed. "Jack was healthy and well, but Smudge had a reputation for being unkind to his children. It's part of the reason why he went out of business eight years ago. He died of sweep's cancer shortly after that."

"What happened to the children?" Mabel asked.

"They were apprenticed to other sweeps, but now that the Chimney Sweepers Regulation Act has been passed, few children work as sweeps anymore. I'm interviewing the other sweeps as I track them down. Jack might have gone to one of them," said Nathan.

"Oh, thank you, Mr. Goulding." Mabel dried her eyes and took the report. "Thank you so very much. This is more than anyone has told me in ten years."

"There is another possibility but there's no evidence for it." Mr Goulding shifted uncomfortably on his feet. He didn't quite meet her eyes when he said "One of the sweeps believes Jack has become part of a gang of child thieves — just something he heard mind — nothing but hearsay.

Mabel's breath hitched, and her grip tightened around the shawl draped over her shoulders. "A thief?" she whispered, the word almost lost in the air. Her heart sank at the thought of her Jack, her sweet boy, turning to a life of crime.

Mr. Goulding looked away, his discomfort clear. "Just hearsay, Mrs. Finch—nothing confirmed."

But Mabel's mind was already spiralling, imagining her son, desperate and alone, driven to steal.

Tears filled her eyes again, blurring her vision. She swallowed hard, trying to steady herself. "Thank you… thank you, Mr. Goulding," she said, her voice wavering. "This is more than anyone has told me in ten years. At least now I have something…"

Nathan stepped closer, his voice gentle. "I'll write as soon as I learn more. I'll do everything I can to find your boy."

Mabel had heard similar promises before, hollow and fleeting. But something in Nathan's eyes made her want to believe, that he meant it.

Percy hurried out of the courthouse, grimacing at the time. The session had run three hours late. He knew that poor Mabel must have gone to the investigator on her own; he guessed he was more likely to find her at the modest inn where they were staying than at the investigator's office.

He'd start there and head to Goulding Investigations if he didn't find her at the inn.

Dismay knotted in his belly, but he knew that Mabel would understand. If any woman could handle the investigator on her own, it was her.

As far as Percy could tell, Mabel wasn't afraid of anything. Especially not when it came to their children.

He turned down a side street to take a shortcut through the type of area where most lawyers seldom set foot, thinking of Jack. The boy's father, Ned, Mabel's late first husband, had been a real beast. But from what Mabel had told him about Jack, he was more like his mother than his drunken, wife-beating father.

Percy's heart ached. Though he'd never had the privilege of meeting Jack, his wife's grief had become his own. He thought of all the things he loved about Maggie and Eddie.

Chief among them were how much the little ones looked and acted like Mabel. Somewhere out there, in this vicious city, there was another piece of Mabel who needed their help.

Oh, Lord, Percy prayed, *help us find sweet Jack.*

He paused at a busy crossing. Heavy wagons and rushing carriages hustled to and fro. The people on the sidewalk cast curious glances at the well-dressed man standing among them instead of riding in a carriage.

Horse manure littered the cobblestones, and Percy glanced up and down, waiting for the traffic to clear.

Sudden movement on his left made him spin around.

"Sorry, sir. I didn't mean to startle you." A young street urchin doffed his cap, perhaps thirteen or fourteen years old. The boy had hair so grimy Percy couldn't ascertain its colour, but his eyes were gentle. "Sweep the crossing for you, sir?"

Percy didn't mind stepping around a few manure piles. He lived on a farm, after all, and loved the farm life as much as his wife did. But the poor lad's shoulders were bony beneath his ragged coat, which was several inches too small. His pinched, pale face spoke of a lifetime of starvation.

"Yes, thank you," said Percy kindly, not wanting to degrade the boy's dignity. "That would be kind."

"Yes, sir. Quick as they come, sir, I'll make sure you get across without a speck of dust on you." The boy touched his cap again, and as the traffic cleared, he strode onto the street. His broom was shabby and suffering much wear, but the boy worked it across the cobbles with a good will.

Percy knew he should drum up the energy to have a kindly conversation with the sweeper, but his heart was with Mabel.

He hurried across the street, thinking of her, and stopped on the pavement to root around in his pockets. The boy licked his lips in anticipation. His bony hands trembled on his broom handle.

"Thank you very much," said Percy, withdrawing half-a-crown from his purse.

He pressed it into the boy's palm. The sweeper gasped, his eyes very wide. His hand darted to his pocket before he hesitated.

"Sir, are you sure you've given me the right coin?" the boy asked. He held out his grubby hand, the coin resting on his skin. "This is half-a-crown."

Percy smiled and laid a hand on his shoulder. "Sleep warm tonight. I wish I could do more." He turned and strode away, feeling the child's shock as he moved away.

There was so much heart-breaking need in this city. Maybe once they'd found their little Jack, Percy and Mabel could do more to help the poor.

Chapter Ten

Half-a-crown. *Half-a-crown!*

To Jack, it was an unimaginable amount of money these days. He'd eaten his fill of rabbit stew the night before, and bread-and-butter this morning from a vendor who also sold hot tea. He sipped the tea now, hands wrapped around his tin cup against the cold. It even had milk in it, and Jack had enough money to replace his broom's entire brush, buy new blankets (the ones he'd taken from Liz's crew had been stolen last winter), and eat for another day or two.

The feeling of knowing where his next meal would come from was buoyant and wonderful. He all but danced down the sidewalk, heading at last for the workhouse. He'd spent the past few weeks so busy trying to earn money and survive that it had been nearly a month since he'd last been there.

And that time, he hadn't seen Beryl.

The thought curdled in his stomach, a quiet dread he'd been pushing down for weeks. He must have missed her in the exercise yard. There were many girls, and they'd been rushing inside to get away from a storm. He simply hadn't spotted her in the crowd. He'd had to rush off to get out of the rain himself before they were all inside.

She was all right. She was there. He'd see her in a moment.

Jack had a skip in his step as he approached the workhouse, its stern shape looming against the grey sky. He quickened as he neared the exercise yard where the young girls went out at this time every morning. Sipping his tea, he dodged behind his usual pillar and peered around the corner.

Little girls huddled in the cold wind, listlessly playing with rocks and sticks in the bare yard. The older ones talked quietly as they sat with their backs to the wall. Beryl was among those older ones now—she'd be about twelve—and Jack anxiously scanned their faces, searching.

Nowhere did he see the beacon of her bright red hair.

He searched again. Maybe she'd had lice, maybe they'd cut off all her beautiful hair. But after ten minutes, the tin cup fell from his numb fingers.

There was no longer any doubt. Beryl wasn't there.

Fire burned in Jack's chest with every breath. He struggled against it, ignoring the irritation in his throat as he tried to smile brightly at the handsome gentleman rushing along the pavement. Despite the weakness that made his limbs ache, Jack cheerily raised his broom.

"Good morning to you, sir!" he cried. "Sweep the—"

Inevitably, the cold air pierced his sore throat. A cough assailed him, and he tried to hold it back, but couldn't. The devastating coughing fit made his sore chest flame with agony, and he bent double, hacking and wheezing, retching with the phlegm that clogged his lungs.

The gentleman sneered and darted away. Jack's heart sank through his boots as more people gave him a wide berth; several crossed without a sweeper, a whole knot of others waited for the adult sweeper to get to work. None dared approach Jack.

They knew the same thing he did: that he was sick.

The coughing left him weak and shaky. He reeled over to a nearby bench and sank down on it, breathing hard.

"Oi!" an angry voice growled.

Jack looked up. A nearby shopkeeper brandished his broom.

"Clear off!" he barked. "You're scaring off the customers."

Jack knew that to protest would only lead to a beating. He stumbled to his feet and staggered away, chest burning, until he found an unoccupied alley. There, he sank to the ground and leaned his head against the wall, breathing hard.

Beryl wasn't in the workhouse. He didn't know where she was.

Of all the afflictions with which he suffered at that moment, Beryl's absence was still the worst. He hadn't realized how much seeing her had buoyed him, even if he never spoke to her, even if he ran away on the few occasions when she spotted him. She had been his hope and joy. And now he didn't know where she was.

Maybe she had been apprenticed out to an even worse fate, like he had. Or maybe she was—

He wouldn't let the word *dead* cross his mind. His hands clenched on his broom.

Beryl couldn't be dead, because if she was, he'd have nothing left. He hadn't eaten in two days; his coughs drove clients away on the crossing. The splendid half-a-crown that the nice gentleman had given him was long gone. He still looked out for the nice gentleman, but he had had a country way about him, and Jack hadn't seen him in the last three weeks. He must have been from out of town. His presence had been a miracle.

But now Jack was all out of miracles.

The thump of footsteps caught his attention. He looked up as a heavy, paunchy man strode past, laughing at something his friend had said. The chain of a silver pocket watch dangled from his lapel, tantalizingly unguarded.

It would be so easy to jump up and quietly follow him. Jack knew he could snatch that pocket watch in less than a minute, and it would feed him for over a week. Sticky buns, beef stew, apple pie... His starved stomach ached at the thought.

Jack closed his eyes and stayed where he was. No. He'd done enough evil things in his life. Beryl would be ashamed of him.

Mama would be ashamed of him.

In this private moment, Jack allowed the tears to sting his eyes at the thought of her soft hands and laughing voice. She had to still be out there somewhere.

He imagined her searching for him, tracking him through the city. He imagined her crying his name. Oh, the day that they found one another, he would run into her arms. She would hold him as they wept with joy...

The daydream was so vivid that Jack could almost feel her arms around him. But when he opened his eyes, he was all alone in the cold, damp alley.

Fever turned Jack's vision hazy. The day looked cold, but he felt on fire, and his breath steamed as he peered across the street. He clutched his broom with both hands, fiercely resisting the urge to lean on it. It would ruin the twigs.

Jack had no money for food or medicine, let alone replacing those.

He shuffled nearer to the crossing, ignoring the way that the simple movement made his lungs burn, and stood at its edge with trembling determination. Sixpence... tuppence... even ha'penny would lend him a scrap of life. He could get a heel of stale bread for a farthing.

Normally, the thought of stale bread was enough to make him salivate. Yet now, his stomach lurched. Jack couldn't remember the last time he hadn't been hungry.

Am I dying? he wondered.

His aching muscles and blazing lungs made him fear that it was true.

The other side of the crossing seemed busier than this one. He stumbled across, head low, clearing his throat with every breath in an effort to avoid the horrid, damp coughs that scared customers away. Instead, he plastered on a bright smile as he eased his way to the corner, where a cabbie stood warming his hands under his arms beside a tired-looking old cab horse.

"Mornin' to you, Guv," he said.

The cabbie's eyes narrowed, and he turned slightly away.

Jack wondered if the word *death* was written across his forehead. The cabbie seemed to fear it was catching.

He twirled his broom, trying to look energetic and ready for action. The movement made his shoulders sting, and he stopped, wincing. A pang ran through his chest. He struggled to stop it, but a spluttering cough escaped.

"Go away," the cabbie growled.

Jack moved a couple of yards down the curb from the cabbie, but stopped when he heard the brisk clopping of feet approaching. He looked up hopefully as a well-dressed young lady approached, her big skirt bouncing, suggesting money for hoops and petticoats—money, perhaps, for a poor crossing-sweeper.

The cabbie, too, brightened. "Mornin', miss!" he called. "Take you anywhere you like. Know the city like the back of my hand."

The lady smiled and quickened her step. Jack spotted some straw blowing across the sidewalk from the cab horse's nosebag and stepped forward, raising his broom to clear her way in the hopes of a tuppence or so. But he moved too quickly. This time, he couldn't hold back the coughs. They racked him, shuddered through him, shook every joint in his body. He doubled over, hacking, and couldn't blame the young lady when she backed away with widening eyes.

"No, miss!" the cabbie cried. "It's all right. It's—"

The lady didn't spare him or Jack a second glance. She turned on her heel and hurried away, glancing over her shoulder from time to time as if to make sure Jack wasn't chasing her.

"Now look what you've done, you filthy wretch," the cabbie yelled.

Jack raised his head. "What?"

"I told you to clear off," the cabbie snapped. "Get out of here! You're scaring off my customers!"

Jack edged away, but he knew that he'd have better luck on this side of the street than the other at this time of morning. "I only want to sweep the crossing for people."

"I don't care what you want," the cabbie snapped. "Go away!" He waved his arms, making the horse toss his head and roll his eyes.

"You're scaring your horse," Jack rasped through his swollen throat.

"Don't talk to me about my horse. Get lost!" the cabbie barked.

Jack retreated a few more yards, coughing as he went. His blazing chest felt so congested that he seemed to be breathing through a straw, sucking in labouring breaths as his lungs and ribs spasmed and shuddered. He leaned against a streetlamp, retching with agony and discomfort.

His limbs trembled as he raised his head, despairingly scanning the street for customers. But there were none—none within ten yards of him, in any case. Several people gave him wide-eyed looks, then dodged across the street several yards away from the crossing. A few gave the cabbie longing glances before hurrying down the block to the other cab on the corner.

Jack's stomach dropped with dismay, but before he could do anything about it, a hand landed on his shoulder.

"I told you to go!" the cabbie thundered.

The rage in his voice terrified Jack. He fell back with a cry, raising his broom to defend himself, and the cabbie's strong hands closed around the stick.

"No!" Jack wailed.

He clung to the broom with all his strength, but the cabbie was strong and healthy, and he yanked the broomstick effortlessly through Jack's fingers.

"No! Please!" Jack cried. "Please, it's all I have!"

"I told you to leave," the cabbie sneered. "You should have listened."

He lowered the broom and raised his knee.

"No!" Jack sobbed, and then another coughing fit consumed him. He could barely see through streaming eyes as the cabbie braced the precious broomstick over his knee and snapped it with one careless movement.

Jack's knees gave way. He fell to the sidewalk, sobbing, as the cabbie threw the shattered broom on the ground in front of him.

"Now you have no reason to be on this crossing," the cabbie hissed. "Take your illness elsewhere, you wretched urchin."

He was right. He'd shattered the last of Jack's hope. Trembling with weakness, Jack reeled to his feet and staggered away, tears stinging on his burning cheeks.

Jack had seldom seen the front of the workhouse. He always approached from behind, where Beryl's exercise yard used to be, and at first today was the same; he wandered by, leaning against the palisades from time to time when his strength abandoned him, and gazed into the yard. The girls were out there, some sitting, some playing, as always. And there was no sign of Beryl.

With painful slowness, Jack stumbled up to the workhouse's facade and stared at the towering building with its stern, heartless lines and its narrow, barred door. He wrapped his arms around himself, supporting his aching chest, and stared at it. Though it was ten years since Mama had brought him here, Jack remembered those few minutes with terrifying clarity. He remembered the scary lady staring at them while they bathed. He remembered the scratchy, hateful workhouse clothes.

He remembered another scary person coming in to drag him away from Mama, and he'd never forget her sobbing apology as he was dragged away.

The memory drenched his blood with ice. He froze in place, staring at that barred door.

The workhouse was his only hope of survival now, slim though it was. They would have to put him in the infirmary... they would have to feed him. He could claw his way back to life in there, and yet, knowing that, he couldn't get his feet to move. They remained rooted to the spot as though he'd been encased in ice.

He stood there for a long time, staring and staring. It was only when a scruffy porter opened the door and yelled, "Oi, are you coming in or not?" that Jack realized he would rather die where he stood than set foot back in that place.

He ignored the porter. Instead, he turned, shuffling in agony, and plodded down the street. He chose no direction except away from the workhouse. He had no goal except to find somewhere out of the wind to die.

Chapter Eleven

The streets around Jack swam with fever. Strange shapes squirmed in the shadows; people's faces melted and swirled in his delirious vision. He stumbled down the sidewalk, completely lost although his subconscious told him that he knew these streets.

One of the swimming faces cursed at him and gestured angrily, raising a hand as though to strike. Jack reeled into the street. Brakes screeched, hooves clattered, and somebody else cursed as well. Jack barely saw the carriage as it swerved to avoid him and then thundered on. He tripped on the curb and fell on his hands and knees, and pedestrians darted around him, giving him furious and frightened glances.

"Come on, my Little Jack." A melodic laugh rippled through the air.

Slowly, Jack raised his head, and she was standing there in front of him in all her splendour. Mama wore a simple work dress with stains on the apron. Her hands were red and calloused, but he knew that their touch was feather-light.

"Come on, silly," said Mama. "It's time to go." She was radiant, her face glowing gold in the evening light.

"Mama," Jack whispered.

A man passing by glanced at him and darted away in fear.

Jack swayed to his feet and stood there, shaking. Mama kept her hand held out, her eyes sparkling, gentle and pure.

"You're wasting time, Jack-Jack," she said. "We have to go."

"All right, Mama," Jack croaked.

He took a staggering, stumbling step forward, then another. He didn't ask where they were going; in the fevered whirl of his mind, the question didn't exist. All he knew was that he had to follow Mama, and that he would follow her anywhere, anywhere.

"That's right, love." Mama's eyes shone. "Well done, Jack-Jack. Keep coming."

Jack's knees buckled. He fell to the grimy sidewalk; a shopkeeper shouted something from the window, but Mama's soft voice drowned him out.

"Get up, Little Jack. You have to get up."

Jack didn't question her. Somehow, he rose, every aching, failing muscle stinging in protest. Then he stumbled forward another step... another.

"That's right, love," said Mama. "You're almost there."

Jack swayed and grabbed a tree branch to stay upright. He didn't know how it had happened, but he was suddenly in a garden. Maybe he was at Heaven's gates. Maybe Mama had died in the workhouse after all. He hardly cared; she was here now, when he needed her most. Maybe they could be together again.

Grass crunched beneath his feet. Bushes, branches, something tickled his cheeks with incredible softness. He thought maybe it was Mama's fingers, but suddenly he couldn't see her. Panic briefly gripped him.

"Over here, Jack-Jack," Mama called.

Jack slowly turned and spotted her. She stood in a corner by a wall... a church wall. He was in a church garden. Birds chirped; otherwise, there was silence.

"Come and lie down, my love." Mama sat on the soft grass in the lee of the wall, out of the wind. "Come and rest."

Rest. That was all Jack wanted. He somehow made it the last few steps to Mama and then fell to the ground on his side, but his head landed in her warm, soft lap. She stroked his hair as he lay there, his breaths labouring, stinging in his burning lungs. The lullaby she hummed had no words, yet instantly lulled him to a warm, peaceful sleep.

Light, soft hands. Mama was touching his face. A cool towel touched his forehead. She hummed as she worked, not the same lullaby, but a pleasant song. A hymn, perhaps. It was very nice.

The voices drifted in and out of focus through the blurs and darkness that made up his world.

"He's burning up."

"Poor mite. Where did he come from?"

Then movement, and pain that cast him into darkness, which ebbed again to the sensation of softness and more voices.

"He's been on the streets a long time, Reverend. I'm not sure…"

"I'll stop you right there, doctor. Tell me what he needs."

"It may be consumption. It may be no use."

"We are unafraid to pray for a miracle."

Water dripping. Bitter liquid rolling down his throat; he wanted to spit, but the soft voice he thought was his mother's said, "Come on, lad, drink up," and he found the strength to choke it down.

Then… a cessation of pain. He could almost open his eyes the next time.

"Doctor, his fever's broken."

"By Jove, Reverend, you're right. I don't believe it!"

A soft laugh. "I do."

Then, there was rest. Long, wonderful, peaceful rest.

It could have been hours or weeks later that Jack opened his eyes and gazed up at a white ceiling bordered with floral wallpaper. It was a little faded, but spotlessly clean. He lay very still, breathing quietly. He couldn't remember the last time he'd woken up to gaze at a ceiling rather than a bare roof or the stars.

His hands felt stiff when he tried to move them. Something rustled beneath them, and when Jack stirred, he realized that his head rested on a real pillow. He stirred again, surprised, and winced when an old, stiff pain rushed through him. The sensation elicited a quiet groan that he tried to stifle.

Someone moved near him; a dress rustled. Jack's heart leaped with hope. Suddenly he remembered Mama finding him, remembered lying with his head in her lap, and he knew that she must be beside him.

"M-Mama," he croaked, and turned his head.

Instantly, fear and disappointment clashed in his chest. There was no sign of his mother. Instead, the woman who sat in the chair beside the bed was older and heavyset, with white streaks in her dark hair. She held a white shirt in her lap and a sewing needle in one hand, and surprise made her eyes wide and round.

Jack glanced around the room. It held only a dresser and a door, apart from the bed and chair. The door might be locked, but there was a window also. He wondered if he'd have the strength to pull himself through it and flee.

"There, there, my lamb," said the woman, with sudden and unexpected kindness.

The surprise left her eyes; they creased in a smile instead. She laid her sewing aside and reached for his arm. Jack flinched out of habit, but when her bony hand rested on his arm, it was shockingly gentle.

"You're safe now," said the woman. "You're all right."

Jack's fear slowly ebbed. "Wh-where am I?" he whispered.

"You're in the vicarage at Saint Jude's," the woman told him. "Nobody's going to hurt you. Even the doctor says you'll be all right now, my lamb."

"The vicarage," Jack croaked.

"That's right. Reverend Samuel found you curled up on the grass outside the church, you poor thing, already half dead and frozen. It's a blessed miracle you're still with us, my lamb, a blessed miracle." The woman squeezed his arm.

"Did… did anyone see… my mama?" Jack whispered.

The woman shook her head. "You were all alone, dear."

Jack closed his eyes. She had been nothing but a fever dream… yet a fever dream that had led him to safety.

"What's your name, little lamb?" the woman asked.

"Jack," he croaked. "Jack Finch."

"Rest now, Jack," said the woman. "I'm Mrs. Brownstone, and I'll take good care of you. Don't worry about a thing, now."

She wasn't Mama, but he believed her soft voice, and sank quietly into sleep.

The vicarage was a space clearly designed for a family with children. Sunlight from the large window filled the dining room, which held a table that could easily seat six or eight. The sideboard was long enough to accommodate a whole array of dishes, but was now spotlessly clean and empty. Instead, a few dishes rested on the table, where Reverend Samuel sat at the head. Two more places were set on his left and right.

Jack hesitated before entering the room, the way he'd done for the past several days—ever since he was well enough to come downstairs for breakfast. But Mrs. Brownstone gave his arm a gentle squeeze, and he shuffled into the room.

Reverend Samuel looked up from the paper and folded it onto his lap.

The distinguished-looking young man had long, brown sideburns and intelligent blue eyes that lit up instantly with his smile.

"Ah, good morning, Jack," he said. "You look much better."

"He's got real colour in his cheeks this morning, doesn't he, Reverend?" Mrs. Brownstone patted Jack's cheek with pride. "Now we need to get some meat on those bones."

Samuel chuckled. "That must be why you made a mountain of toast this morning."

"It'll put hairs on his chest," said Mrs. Brownstone briskly.

Jack sank into the chair at the table, still feeling awkward. He hadn't eaten at a table with a knife and fork since the workhouse; even there, children often ate with their hands, terrified that their food might be stolen.

"Let's say grace," said Samuel. He bowed his head and prayed sincerely and simply, "For what we are about to receive, may the Lord make us truly thankful. Amen."

"Amen," said Mrs. Brownstone.

"Amen," said Jack, hardly knowing what that meant.

Mrs. Brownstone shovelled buttered toast onto his plate. Jack's appetite had returned fiercely after his illness, and he couldn't stop himself from grasping the first piece and biting into it.

"Look at the appetite on this boy!" Mrs. Brownstone laughed. "Isn't that lovely to see?"

Samuel smiled. "Indeed. I'm very pleased you're so well again, Jack. We all prayed so hard for you."

Gulping down his toast, Jack didn't know what to say. His toes curled inside his slippers—which had been waiting for him at the foot of his bed that morning—as he thought of the person he truly was. Surely, Samuel thought he was some poor little street urchin. He thought he was doing a good deed.

He had no idea that the boy he harboured under his own roof was a thief and a traitor besides.

Jack ate slowly, saying nothing, as Samuel and Mrs. Brownstone chatted about people whose names he didn't recognize. He guessed they were members of the congregation; Samuel seemed to know the names of everyone, as well as their children and families, their joys and woes. It made Jack's shame grow all the more. Why had Samuel never asked him where he came from?

"I think I'll go and see Mrs. Smythe now," Samuel was saying, dabbing his lips with a napkin. "Thank you for an excellent breakfast, Mrs. Brownstone."

"I'm sure Mrs. Smythe will be glad to see you, the poor dear. She's been so terribly lonely since her husband died." Mrs. Brownstone rose and gathered the dishes; Jack had polished his plate. "Would you like another boiled egg, Jack, my lamb?"

"Now, now, Mrs. Brownstone," said Samuel, smiling, "you know that the doctor said not to give him too much rich food."

"All right, then." Mrs. Brownstone sighed. "Well, do you feel up to a little turn about the garden, Jack? The fresh air will do you a world of good, my lamb. You look strong enough today."

"If it's not too much trouble," said Jack timorously.

"It's no trouble at all, dear," said Mrs. Brownstone.

She made him believe it, too; Samuel left a few minutes later, and Mrs. Brownstone led Jack outside, her hand resting firmly over his as he leaned on her arm. The little woman was elderly but stout, and she marched outside at a brisk pace.

Spring's colours had brought vibrant green to the church garden. Sprinklings of flowers began to bloom in the beds around the large building, and though the lawns badly needed cutting, they were richly green.

With a tall hedge separating the church from the street, Jack could barely believe that the cruel city lay just across the hedge. It was so quiet and peaceful in the garden with his feet sinking into the grass and the unusual, warm sunshine pouring onto his skin.

"There you are, my lamb." Mrs. Brownstone beamed. "That's much better, isn't it?"

"It's very nice," said Jack. "Thank you."

Mrs. Brownstone patted his hand. "Tell me, my dear, when did you lose your mama?"

Jack looked away. "I thought she led me here," he said softly, "but it was all a dream. I haven't seen her in ten years, Mrs. Brownstone."

"You poor lamb. Have you been all on your own all this time?" she asked.

Jack quietly nodded; he couldn't bear to tell her that he'd been part of a gang of thieves before now.

"Poor lamb," said Mrs. Brownstone again.

"It felt so real," Jack admitted. "I heard her calling me to come here. She told me to lie down in that corner where the reverend found me."

Mrs. Brownstone squeezed his hand. "The Lord does wonderful things sometimes, my lamb. He'll use anything He needs to call us gently to Himself."

Jack only vaguely remembered the chapel lessons from his time in the workhouse. He knew that people worshiped this Lord that Mrs. Brownstone spoke of, but never had he heard someone speak of Him in such gentle and admiring towns, with such awe and real love. He wondered why the Lord she spoke of would want to call anyone—least of all Jack—to Himself.

"Look at that." Mrs. Brownstone stopped and shaded her eyes as she gazed up at the church. "Isn't it lovely?"

Jack's response froze in his throat. He stared at the steeple, the familiar shape burned into his memory, and his heart thudded so wildly that he feared it might break free of his ribs.

He remembered the snorts of terrified horses, the yells of children. He remembered the carriage driver's cry.

Get out, m'lady! Get out!

Then the panicked scream of an old woman falling to the ground, and her shivering as Finn snatched her necklaces over her head.

It had happened only a few yards from where Jack now stood. He had hurt and terrified that poor, harmless old lady right here, in front of this church. The vicar who ran out to help her had been Reverend Samuel. He remembered now, the sideburns, the wide, frightened eyes. He remembered everything.

"Jack!" cried Mrs. Brownstone, clutching him. "You've gone as white as a sheet!"

Jack couldn't utter a word. Horror crushed him like a gigantic fist.

"Come, come, my boy," said Mrs. Brownstone. "Let's take you back inside, poor lamb."

But as she hurried him back into the vicarage, Jack knew that he was no lamb. He was no innocent victim of this cruel city. He was the cruel, heartless thief who'd terrorized that old woman.

No amount of regret could ever cleanse him of that. Nothing could ever make him worthy of these good people and their kindness.

The weight of his guilt felt heavy enough to kill him. And so, late that night, when Mrs. Brownstone and Samuel lay asleep, Jack slipped through the front door and out into the streets where he belonged.

The wind was miserable. Mrs. Brownstone had given Jack an old coat of Reverend Samuel's; he would have left it at the vicarage, but they had burned his old, filthy clothes, and he had no choice. He supposed it still made him a thief.

Yet he was glad of the thick fabric that offered some protecting against the biting wind that howled so savagely down the street. With the collar turned up, he still felt nips of cold against his nose and cheeks. He kept his hands tucked into the pockets as he stood on the street corner, watching the crowd hurry past.

Last night had been miserable. Jack hadn't realized how wonderful it was to sleep in a bed with sheets, blankets, and a pillow until he'd experienced it again. One night on the streets was enough to make his recovering body ache fiercely with every step. Perhaps he would find a more sheltered place tonight.

He extended a hand as a gentleman strode past, his pockets jingling with coins. "Alms?" he whispered. "Spare alms for the poor?"

The gentleman shot him a scathing look, then crossed the street and hurried away.

So it had been since Jack left the vicarage two nights ago. His coat was too nice to belong to a beggar. Every person who passed him, judged him unworthy.

They were right. Who was he to stand here with his hands open, asking for free gifts from the people whose watches and money he'd stolen? He had betrayed them, and now he expected them to care for him. It was no wonder that none dared stop to look.

His hands fell to his sides, and the weight of Jack's failures hung on his shoulders as though he was dragging a ship's anchor. He pressed his hands to his face, struggling to hold back tears.

"Jack!"

The clear voice cut through the fog of despair in his mind. He felt leaping hope—and then, instantly, horror.

The voice belonged to Reverend Samuel.

Jack's head snapped up, and he instantly spotted the black cassock swirling as Samuel all but ran towards him. Heads turned and people stared in surprise as Samuel pushed through the crowd, arms outstretched.

"Jack!" he cried again. "Oh, praise the Lord, there you are!"

Jack hesitated, wanting to flee, but his still-weak limbs gave him no choice but to stay rooted to the spot as Samuel rushed to him. He tensed as the vicar reached him and pulled him into a crushing embrace that smelled of the polish used at the church's lectern.

"My poor boy, you must be so cold." Samuel squeezed him briefly, then let him go. "Come, come. Please, you must come out of the cold."

"Sir—" Jack croaked.

"This is no good for your chest, Jack." Samuel gently took his arm.

Jack resisted as he tried to tug him down the sidewalk.

Samuel looked up, releasing his grip. He would force him nowhere, Jack realized. It was not in the vicar's gentle nature to compel him to do anything.

"I'm sorry if I came across over-zealous," said Samuel. "I know you must have a reason to have left; I will hear it out with my all my heart, only come out of the wind and let me buy you a meal, my dear boy."

Jack's aching stomach won out over his stinging heart. He meekly followed Samuel to a nearby tea-shop, where the waitress stared at them both in confusion, but went to fetch tea and toast in any case. Jack sagged into a chair and stared miserably into his tea as Samuel offered him sugar cubes. He declined them and sipped the hot tea without milk; it scalded all the way down, painful and wonderful in his cold, empty stomach.

"All right," said Samuel, when Jack had slowly finished his tea. "Please. Tell me why you left."

Jack swallowed against the knot in his throat. The tea-shop was nearly empty; only an old gentleman snored in a corner, his newspaper forgotten on the table. The waitress kept her distance from Jack's grimy figure.

"I'm not who you think I am," he croaked. "Sir, Mr. Reverend, I'm not an innocent child you rescued from the street. I don't deserve your kindness."

Samuel tilted his head. "Why do you say that?"

Jack stared into the man's gentle eyes and fleetingly considered saying something untrue, something that would make his failures seem puny. He knew Samuel would be kind to him then.

But what next? Would he go back to the vicarage and eat sardines and boiled eggs every day, knowing that he was a liar as well as a thief?

No. His flaws swelled within him like vomit. There was only one way out.

"I'm a thief," he croaked. "I'm a dirty, rotten thief."

Samuel said nothing, nor did his expression change. If he was angry, he hid it well.

"I ran with a gang of child thieves, but I was a thief even before that," said Jack. "I stole people's purses and pocket watches, their cigar cases, their food... Anything that I could lay my hands on. We stole everything that we needed and many, many things that we didn't need. We stole from old men and women, from children, and from working fathers trying to get home to their families. We stole from shops and carts. We stole from the rich and the poor. We didn't care who we stole from; we took whatever we wanted, and I..." The dark truth escaped. "I enjoyed it. Every minute."

Samuel made no excuses. He merely nodded and sipped his tea, and the silence invited Jack to continue.

"It's worse than that," he said. "I was just a little boy when I stole for the first time, and that same night, I abandoned my best friend." His breath hitched. "Beryl was the closest thing I had to family. I hurt her, I frightened her, and then..." The shame almost crushed him. "Then I left her. I saw her in the workhouse after that, but I was too much of a coward to go up to her. Now I don't know if I'll ever see her again." His voice broke.

Samuel studied him in kind silence. Jack couldn't understand why the vicar wasn't shouting and screaming for him to leave at once.

"Sir," Jack croaked, "do you remember a day, almost two years ago, when an old woman was attacked in front of the church?"

Samuel nodded. "I remember it well. Mrs. Penelope Johnson. Some children frightened her horses, caused a commotion, and others took her purse and jewellery." His tone was calm, a simple statement of facts, without a trace of judgment.

Jack took a deep breath, his heart pounding. "I was there. I was one of them."

Samuel's expression softened, his gaze steady and gentle, but he didn't seem surprised. "I know, Jack."

Jack blinked, disbelief flooding his face. "You knew?"

"I recognized you," Samuel said quietly. "It was a chaotic day, one that's hard to forget."

"You... you knew who I was when you took me in?" Jack stammered, his voice breaking.

Samuel nodded again. "Yes, I did."

"But why?" Jack asked, his confusion evident in his eyes. "Why would you help me, knowing what I'd done?"

Samuel stirred his tea slowly, as if choosing his words with care. "Everyone has a past, Jack. We've all done things we regret. But I've also seen people change. That day, I saw fear in your eyes, but I also saw something else—something that made me believe you could be more than the mistakes you've made."

Jack's shoulders sagged, weighed down by guilt and shame. "But... I'm a thief," he muttered. "I've done terrible things. I hurt people."

Samuel leaned forward, his voice calm but firm. "You were a thief, Jack. But that's not all you are. You don't have to be defined by your worst moments. You can choose who you want to be from here on out. That's in your hands."

Jack's eyes filled with tears. He hadn't expected this, hadn't expected such understanding. "I won't steal from you, sir," he blurted out, his voice thick with emotion. "Never again."

Samuel's smile was small, but genuine. "I believe you, Jack. I've seen the effort you've put in, the way you've tried to make amends. That shows character, and it matters more than anything you've done before."

Jack nodded slowly, struggling to hold back his tears. "Thank you, sir... for giving me a chance. I don't deserve it, but... thank you."

Samuel reached out and gave Jack's shoulder a reassuring squeeze. "You're here because you've earned that chance. Remember, the past is just a part of your story, not the whole of it. Now, let's head home, shall we?"

Home. The word felt foreign, almost surreal, but also strangely comforting. Jack wiped his eyes with the back of his hand, feeling a rush of emotions—relief, gratitude, and a faint, fragile hope. He followed Samuel out of the church, stepping into the cool evening air, feeling for the first time that maybe, just maybe, he could find his place in the world.

As they walked, Samuel spoke again, his voice soft but encouraging. "And remember, Jack, you're not alone. You've got people here who care about you. You've got a future to look forward to."

Jack nodded, a small, tentative smile breaking through. "I'll do my best, sir. I promise."

"I know you will, Jack. I know you will."

Part Five

Chapter Twelve

One Year Later

Whitewash dribbled down the church wall. Jack carefully caught it with the tip of his paintbrush, then smoothed it away in gentle strokes. He balanced on the top of the ladder, humming a soft, wordless tune as he worked, a habit he'd developed over the past year. The familiar melody helped keep his mind focused, a comforting distraction from the thoughts that often lingered.

He glanced at the sky, realizing he still needed to polish the organ pipes before nightfall. They had to be gleaming for the next day's service. Picking up his pace, Jack carefully worked the brush into the top corner of the church wall, ensuring every spot was covered with fresh whitewash.

Satisfied with his progress, he climbed down the ladder and wiped his brush clean on the edge of the paint tin. After rinsing the brush, he carried the tin back to the garden shed.

"Are you finished, Jack?" Samuel's voice called from inside the church.

Jack shut the shed door and stepped into the doorway of the church office, where Samuel was busy sorting through a pile of papers.

"Yes, sir," Jack replied. "The painting's done. I'll start polishing the organ pipes now."

"Already! You're a hard worker," Samuel said with a warm smile. "The church has never looked better since you became our groundskeeper. We're lucky to have you."

"No, sir," Jack said, touching his forelock out of habit. "I'm lucky to be here."

Samuel shook his head. "I just wish we could pay you what you're worth, Jack."

Jack smiled. "I have all I need staying here with you, Reverend. That's more than enough for me."

"You're worth more, though," Samuel insisted. "Don't forget that."

Jack chuckled softly. "Let me get to those pipes."

He retrieved a cloth and some polish from the broom cupboard and carried his ladder into the church. He enjoyed the quietness of the empty sanctuary, the sense of peace that filled the space when it was just him working. There were no grand decorations here; every spare penny went to help the needy. But Jack took pride in keeping the place tidy. The large windows were always clear, letting in the sunlight, and the pews were polished and ready for the congregation. Mrs. Brownstone made sure fresh flowers adorned the lectern.

Jack set up the ladder and climbed carefully, beginning to polish the brass organ pipes with swift, steady movements. He continued to hum, the sound of his own voice keeping him company in the solitude.

As he polished, a familiar thought crept into his mind, one he had carried with him for months. "Beryl," he murmured under his breath, "I hope you're out there somewhere, safe and sound."

He had whispered her name countless times, each time feeling the same ache in his chest. He missed her terribly. Was she okay? Was she alone, like he had been before he came here?

What could he do for her now?

If he ever found her, Jack vowed silently, he would do anything to help her. But for now, he had to keep going, keep working, and keep hoping.

Though Jack had lived in the orderly calm of the vicarage for a full year, he still felt slightly surprised every evening as he finished bathing and slipped into his comfortable, warm nightclothes. They rustled on his freshly washed skin, feeling inexpressibly soft and clean. Such things were rarities in the workhouse and non-existent on the streets. Jack had never felt so spoiled before now.

He smoothed his damp hair back and moved to the edge of his bed. A small, well-worn bible lay on his nightstand, and the bed was neatly made with crisp sheets. Jack turned down the covers, but before sliding his tired limbs between them after a long day of work in the church, he sat down on the edge of the bed. He took a deep breath, closing his eyes, letting the quiet of the room settle around him.

"Today was a good day," he whispered softly, recalling the kindness of Reverend Samuel and the gentle encouragement from Mrs. Brownstone. He whispered a quiet prayer for the frail old man from their congregation, hoping he would find comfort and strength. Jack's gaze dropped to his hands, and he rubbed his thumb over his knuckles, feeling the familiar ache.

"Beryl," he murmured, his voice barely audible, "I hope you're safe wherever you are. I hope I find you someday." His thoughts drifted to his mother, the memory of her face hazy yet so dear to him. "Mama... I miss you so much. I hope you're all right, wherever you are. I wish I could see you again." Before he drifted to sleep he said a prayer for them both.

Mabel sat on the edge of her bed, her hands resting in her lap. Her eyes were misty, her thoughts far away. "I miss him so much," she whispered into the stillness of the room. "Every day, I wonder where he is, what he's doing. I just want to hold him again, see him again." She stood and moved to the window, her voice soft and full of longing. "Jack, wherever you are, I hope you're safe. I hope you feel loved. And I hope, someday, we'll be together again."

Across the room, Percy was lounging against the pillows, engrossed in a novel under the soft glow of the gas lamp. He looked up when Mabel moved, a gentle smile on his face, though it wavered when he noticed the sadness in her eyes.

"Mae?" he asked gently. "What's the matter? Come back to bed."

"Oh It's nothing, my dear." Mabel hastily brushed away the tears and pulled the curtain closed before slipping back into bed next to Percy.

He took her hand as she slid between the sheets. "Mr. Goulding is making a little progress, love. He's doing so much better than the other investigators. He'll find Little Jack."

Mabel mutely nodded. It was true; Nathan Goulding had tirelessly tracked down every tidbit of information he could find about Jack, yet those scraps still seemed terribly sparse to Mabel.

"His last information only goes back four years," said Percy encouragingly. "He's tracked down six years of Jack's life in the last two. Maybe, in a few more months, we'll find our little boy."

"Maybe," Mabel croaked, and her voice cracked.

"Oh, Mae." Percy squeezed her hand.

"I can't imagine it, Percy," Mabel whispered. "You know what Mr. Goulding said that one of those sweeps said Jack had become a thief. A thief! My poor little boy, a thief!"

"I know it's terrible, love, but remember he also said there's no evidence for it," Percy murmured.

Mabel's lower lip trembled. "He would never do such a thing unless he had no choice. What… what happened to my baby? What drove him to steal? He…" Her voice hitched. "He must be on the streets, Percy. If he was part of a gang of child thieves, then he was on the streets with them." She herself had spent only a few nights on the street, yet the memories terrorized her. How long had her poor child had nowhere to lay his head? Where would he sleep tonight? Was it raining in London?

"We'll find him, Mae," said Percy.

Mabel swallowed. "I hope so."

"We have to entrust him to the Lord," said Percy kindly. "Losing sleep won't help us find him. Mr. Goulding is making progress. He'll keep on looking for Jack."

Mabel sighed and lay down, pulling the covers to her chin. Percy returned to his book, turning the pages with soft, rustling noises that slowly lulled Mabel toward sleep.

"Percy?" she murmured.

"Yes?"

"I don't care if my Little Jack is a thief," she whispered. "All I want is for him to be alive and safe."

Percy bent to kiss her forehead. "I know, my love," he said. "I know."

"I had the most wonderful dream," said Jack.

He stood on a stepladder in the vicarage that Monday afternoon, repairing a hole in the ceiling. One of the congregations' little boys had grown a bit too rambunctious with his top when Mrs. Brownstone was watching him for his mother.

"Oh?" said Mrs. Brownstone across the kitchen, where she was kneading dough for tomorrow's bread. "Do be careful, my lamb. You'll break your neck if you fall off that ladder."

Jack chuckled. "I'm fine, Mrs. Brownstone." He painted over his repairs.

"What was your dream about?" the housekeeper asked.

"It was about my mother," said Jack. "I dreamed that she was praying for me."

Mrs. Brownstone smiled. "I've no doubt she is, my lamb. I know I'm always praying for you."

"Thank you," said Jack.

"You silly boy," Mrs. Brownstone added, the way she always did when she didn't want to cry, and went back to kneading dough.

"What's wrong?" Jack asked, descending the ladder.

"Nothing at all. Now go and wash up," Mrs. Brownstone ordered. "Reverend Samuel will be back any minute for tea."

"Reverend Samuel is already back," the vicar announced, ducking into the kitchen.

"Tea will be ready in a minute, sir," said the housekeeper.

"Thank you, Mrs. Brownstone." Samuel smiled. "Look at that ceiling! Good as new." A troubled expression flashed across his face, quickly replaced by his habitual smile. "Come into the dining room with me for a minute, Jack. There's something I have to discuss with you."

Confused, Jack followed Samuel into the dining room. He glanced at Mrs. Brownstone as he left the kitchen, but she kept her head down, kneading the bread with hard movements as though it had offended her.

"Is everything all right, sir?" Jack asked. "Is... is this about the ceiling? Did I get something wrong?"

"Jack, no. You've done nothing wrong at all." Samuel smiled and laid a hand on Jack's shoulder, though there was some strain around the corners of his eyes. "Have a seat, dear boy."

Jack sank into a chair at the table and Samuel did the same. The vicar steepled his fingers and gazed at Jack for a moment.

"You've been with us a little more than a year now, Jack," he said, "and in that time, you've done our congregation a tremendous service."

"Not as much of a service as you've done for me, sir," said Jack humbly.

"I don't agree, and that's why I need to talk to you," said Samuel. "You have done excellent work. Though we provide you board and lodging, I believe that you have a very bright future ahead of you. You're diligent and hardworking and you truly care about everyone around you. You're about fifteen now, aren't you?"

"Yes, sir. I think so," said Jack.

"On the precipice of becoming a man," said Samuel. "It's time you were given work that paid you, Jack."

Jack hastily shook his head. "I don't need money, sir. I don't need anything. I like it here."

"You may not think so now, my boy." Samuel smiled and laid a hand over Jack's. "But a day might come when you meet a girl who you want to make your wife, and for that, you will need the means to support her and yourself. Don't you want a family someday?"

A blush crept to Jack's cheeks, and he lowered his head. Beryl inexplicably filled his thoughts.

"You have so much to offer the world. I believe you can truly make something of yourself, Lord willing," said Samuel, "and so I've spoken to an old friend—the housekeeper at Ashcroft Manor."

"Where's that, sir?" Jack asked.

"Across London, almost an hour by carriage from here. I've arranged for a good position for you. It doesn't pay much yet, but you'll have your room and board with money to save up, and the opportunity to work yourself up to a higher position," said Samuel.

Jack blinked. "A... a position? A job somewhere far away? I'd have to stay there?"

"That's right. You'd be a stable lad, and your quarters would be right by the stables." Samuel smiled. "I've seen you looking at the carriage horses on Sundays. I know you love them."

Jack ducked his head. It was true, but the thought of leaving Samuel and Mrs. Brownstone made his heart thud heavily in his wrists.

"I won't make you go, Jack." Samuel squeezed his hand. "Our beloved Lord knows that you're a great asset to our church, but I want what's good for you. I believe that this will be best for you. Besides," he added gently, "you are strong and well now, my little foundling, and ready to move on to greater things. Is it not time to do so and make room for another?"

Jack bit his lip. "I know this is a wonderful gift, sir," he said softly. "Thank you."

Samuel smiled. "You're sad to leave us."

"I am," Jack admitted.

"We'll be sad to see you go." Samuel chuckled. "That's why Mrs. Brownstone is attacking that poor, innocent dough with such vigour."

"I heard that!" Mrs. Brownstone yelled from the kitchen.

"But this will be wonderful for you, my boy." Samuel beamed. "You've made such great progress with your reading and writing. You'll be able to send us notes anytime you like, since you'll have a little money to spend. This can be a fantastic thing."

Money to spend. Perhaps, if Jack could give the porter some money at the workhouse, he'd be able to tell Jack what had happened to Beryl. The thought gave a kick of excitement in his chest.

"I'll go, sir. Thank you, sir," said Jack.

"Wonderful." Samuel rose. "I'll write to Mrs. Whitehall at once."

"Sir?" Jack said.

Samuel paused. "Yes?"

"I'll do you proud, sir," said Jack. "I'll do my best. I'll be good and kind and brave and joyful, like the Good Book says."

Samuel beamed. "I know you will."

Chapter Thirteen

The tram ride was unlike anything Jack had experienced before. It was a new-fangled thing, cheaper than a carriage yet still not inexpensive, but the kind congregation had raised the money to send Jack off to Ashcroft Manor in style.

He walked along the street, following directions given by a kindly flower-seller on the corner near the tram station, trying to hold back his tears as he thought about yesterday. It had been his last day at St Lukes. The congregation had gathered around him, offering warm embraces and kind words to him. They'd pressed little gifts into his hands and sent him off with broad smiles and loud congratulations. He had spoken honestly about the mistakes he'd made in his past, and still, they had shown him unexpected kindness, one gruff man saying matter of factly "Ah lad, we do what we must to survive, and no-one can blame ye for that..

There for the grace of God, go I—go all of us. Good luck young Jack. I know ye'll do well and the Lord'll keep ya." Jack had hugged him tight.

Now, he wore new boots and a freshly mended coat thanks to them, and a warm hat covered his ears as he strode toward the manor. "It's the big house on the end," the flower-seller had said. "You can't miss it."

Indeed, Ashcroft Manor was impossible to miss. Its dark grey stone rose sternly above the other houses, looking at the same time older and more grandiose than the houses surrounding it. Rows upon rows of windows presided over three stories, all with symmetrical pillars and decorative masonry. Behind the tall gates in the palisade fence that reminded him painfully of the workhouse, a fountain stood before the great house, with double doors presiding over broad steps.

Jack knew better than to approach through the main gate. Instead, he went around the manor, passing vast lawns that gave way to horse paddocks and a vegetable garden. The servants' entrance was an unassuming iron gate in the wall. He let himself in and followed the path toward the stable yard.

A chilly breeze blew down the yard toward him, scattering bits of straw across the stone paving, and a delicious smell reached Jack's nostrils. It was the smell of horses, he realized.

He remembered watching Charlie shoe the mighty beasts at the smithy when he was a tiny boy while Mama was at work. Charlie used to laugh and tease him and sometimes let him pet the quieter ones, and he'd never forgotten their gentle eyes or grass-scented breath. Something about them always seemed like magic to him.

He felt a sudden kick of excitement. Perhaps this would be as good as Samuel thought.

Jack couldn't resist turning aside when he reached the first stable on his right. The stables were built in a horseshoe shape, with the tack and feed rooms and the stablemaster's cottage on the end and five loose boxes down either side of the yard. The boxes were spacious and airy with half doors for the horses to look out, and Jack now leaned over one half door to peer at the box's occupant. A magnificent chestnut gelding raised his head at Jack's approach, eyes showing the whites with surprise. The beast had a white line down its nose and huge, fiery eyes that regarded Jack with striking intensity.

"Hello, old boy," said Jack. "I'm not here to hurt you." He extended his arm toward the horse and wiggled his fingers, unable to reach the red-gold coat.

"What are you doing?" an angry voice spluttered.

Jack turned and hastily pasted on a broad smile as a scruffy old man strode across the yard toward him. He had heavy brows and a weak chin dusted with steel-coloured stubble. Baleful, narrow-set eyes glared at Jack, bloodshot and yellowed, from either side of a nose that had been broken more than once. He moved with a painful, shuffling limp as though his left hip could hardly bend at all.

"Good morning, sir!" said Jack as brightly as he could. "My name is Jack Finch. Reverend Samuel—"

"That wretched young fool," the man growled, spitting foul-coloured tobacco on the paving.

Jack recoiled. Anger pulsed through him, and he had to bite his tongue to keep from coming to Reverend Samuel's defence.

"Sir, I've been sent here to become the new stable hand," he said. "The housekeeper is expecting me."

"She's just as foolish as your stupid vicar, boy," the man growled.

Jack raised his chin. "All the same, sir, I'd be most pleased if you could direct me as to where I can speak with her."

"Listen to you." The man sneered. "Think you're one of them, do you?"

He jerked his head toward the towering manor behind them. "Think you can come here and act like a toff? Well, you're nothing, boy." He jabbed a finger at him. "Nothing."

"Sir—" Jack began.

"As for the housekeeper," said the man angrily, "there's no need to speak with her. I already know that you're here to work for me."

Jack paused. "For you, sir?"

"That's right. I'm your stablemaster, Silas Thornfield." The man folded his arms.

Jack blinked, fighting sudden dismay. "I'm pleased to meet you, sir."

"You soon won't be," Silas snapped. "Now put your things in the feed room and get started at once. These stables won't muck out themselves."

"Yes, sir. I'll do that, sir," said Jack.

He scampered to the room where he could see bales of straw and sacks of oats, hastily put his bag on the ground, and returned to the yard. Silas pointed imperiously at a wheelbarrow leaning on the wall near the muck heap along with a fork, shovel, and broom.

"Hurry up," he snapped.

"Yes, sir," said Jack.

He'd never cleaned a stable before, but he assumed it couldn't be that difficult. Quickly collecting his tools, he made for the chestnut gelding's stable and let himself in. Immediately, the big animal pinned himself against the wall and snorted, his tail twitching.

"He'll kick you soon as look at you, the stupid nag," growled Silas. "Hit him with the fork if he comes close."

Jack kept a wary eye on the gelding, but couldn't imagine striking that splendid beast with the length of metal he held in his hands. It was incomprehensible. His nose wrinkled as he shut the door behind him.

Silas chuckled. "Stables are good and dirty. Last boy left three days ago."

"The horses have been standing in their filth all that time?" said Jack.

Silas' eyes narrowed. "I need you to understand something, boy," he hissed. He lifted his coat and flattened his rough trousers, revealing a fist-sized indentation in his left hip. "Do you see this?"

Jack gulped. "Yes, sir."

"That's what these wretched beasts will do to you. Kill you soon as look at you." Silas spat again, making the horse's muscles twitch. "Vicious beasts, better off on our plates, but the rich folks like 'em. So don't you go mollycoddling these animals, do you hear? They're not people. They're beasts. You make them do what you want, and you do it hard. Do you hear me? That's how we do it here, and you'll do it the same."

Jack swallowed. "Yes, sir."

"Now finish these stables by lunchtime or you'll be back on the tram to your precious little church full of foolishness before you can say Jack Robinson," Silas snarled, and strode away.

The horse visibly relaxed as Silas stormed off, then snorted when Jack raised the fork.

"It's all right, old boy," said Jack.

But in his heart, he wasn't sure that it was all right at all.

"Stand up!" Silas bellowed, slapping a hard, flat hand against the horse's neck.

The animal jumped, shoes scrabbling on the paving, and rolled its eyes in panic. Silas yanked hard on the rein so that its jaws fell open in protest. "Stand up!" he yelled again.

Shaking, the grey carriage horse froze in its tracks. Silas sneered as he yanked the girth tight around its belly.

"What are you staring at, boy?" he yelled at Jack.

Jack ducked his head. "Nothing, sir. Can I help you, sir?"

"You can't handle this nag. It'll kick you to pieces," Silas barked. "You've only been here a week and you're already getting too big for your boots."

"Yes, sir," said Jack.

He lowered his head as he waited for Silas to back the carriage horse up to the pole. His horse stood quietly, already harnessed, waiting for its team member. The two grey horses matched perfectly; they had to be brothers, Jack guessed, though he wouldn't dare to ask Silas.

Silas shoved the horse into place. "Hurry up, you lazy child," he barked.

"Yes, sir." Jack hastily buckled the horses to the pole. The younger one, which Silas had harnessed, jumped and snorted with every movement.

A coachman strolled into the yard, pulling on white gloves. He wore a powdered wig and a beautiful tailcoat with shiny, polished boots. Silas sneered harder than ever as the coachman approached the carriage.

"What's the matter with Storm?" the coachman asked.

"Nothing. Wretched, violent beast as usual," Silas growled.

The coachman shook his head. "I don't know what you do to these horses, Silas. I can't manage him like that."

Storm tossed his head as if to agree, yanking the reins from Silas' hands.

"Sir, I'll walk with him," Jack offered, "and he'll settle down, I'm sure."

"Yes, you had better do that," said the coachman.

He mounted the carriage with stately movements and gathered up the reins.

"Those reins will be dry, I expect," Silas growled. "Stupid boy didn't oil them properly."

The words stung; Jack had stayed up well past ten to finish oiling the long leather reins.

"They seem fine to me," said the coachman.

"Fool," Silas muttered.

Jack gripped Storm's bridle. The horse's nostrils flared, but he stood still, quivering.

"I'll help you around to the front, sir," said Jack.

"Very well, but stay out of sight," the coachman ordered. "You're not fit to be seen by the master."

"Yes, sir," said Jack. As far as the Ashcroft family was concerned, Jack was to be as invisible as possible. No one who wore anything but livery or a black-and-white uniform was presentable to them.

He kept his head low as he walked beside the carriage horse, soothing the frightened creature as they moved down the path toward the drive in front of the manor. Storm fussed and fretted, and one iron-rimmed hoof descended painfully on Jack's little toe. He bit back his pain and struggled not to grow angry. How could he work for a man who was so cruel to everything he saw? The horses were all afraid of him; he was quick with his fists, too, and Jack had caught many a cuff to the back of his head.

Perhaps he should tell Samuel how Silas treated him. Samuel would help him to find other work, he supposed.

He sighed and prayed quietly. *I'm trying to be patient and faithful, Lord, but it's so hard. Should I go back to the vicarage? But what about the new children*

Samuel said were coming to stay? What will become of them? Dismay washed through him. He had no choice, and he knew it.

Lord, I trust You, he prayed in silence, *yet please, give me strength.*

Limping on his bruised toe, Jack finally reached the front of the manor. By the time the coachman touched the reins, Storm had realized that Silas was nowhere near, and was quite calm.

"Very good. Thank you, boy," said the coachman. "Now hurry off before they see you."

It was too late. Suddenly, the double doors at the top of the steps began to open, and Jack froze.

"Stand behind the horses! Quickly!" the coachman hissed.

A handsome footman left the house first, fully liveried with his hair neatly combed, and strode down the steps to the carriage. He pulled the door open and stood to attention as the master and mistress came outside.

Jack peered underneath Storm's neck at them. He'd never seen Mr. and Mrs. Ashcroft before, but he knew that the two people at the top of the steps had to be them. They wore beautiful clothes; Mr. Ashcroft a black suit, Mrs. Ashcroft a beautiful, hooped gown. They descended regally and approached the carriage.

Mrs. Ashcroft was about to get in when she turned around. "Annabel, darling," she called, "come on."

"Yes, Mother," someone called from the stairs, and a girl a little younger than Jack emerged onto the steps. She was a pale, slender wisp of a child, a bluish tint around her lips, and her grey eyes seemed vast in her pinched face. Jack was startled. He hadn't known that rich children could be sickly, too.

Annabel Ashcroft hesitated at the top of the steps. "Oh, I need your arm, dear," she begged.

Then she was there.

Beryl.

Jack's knees went so weak that he nearly fell to his face. He gasped and clung to Storm's mane, drawing a glare from the coachman, but he didn't notice. At first, he told himself that it was impossible. The girl who held out her arm to Annabel was much too beautifully dressed to be Beryl. Though her dress was nothing like Annabel's, it was sturdy cotton, dyed green.

But it was her. The curls piled neatly on top of her head were the same shade of striking scarlet. There was colour in her cheeks now, making them glow rosily beneath her curls, and when her eyes swept across the carriage, they were exactly the same. Bright blue, bright as jewels.

Jack trembled. She was here. She was really here, Beryl, his Beryl, alive and well and prospering. He gazed at her as she floated down the steps beside Annabel and then got into the carriage with the family, as though she was one of them!

"Move," the coachman hissed.

Jack stumbled backward. The coachman cracked the whip, and the horses passed him with a rattle of hooves and a rumble of wheels. It happened too quickly for him to look into the carriage and see her fly past.

It was a good thing, Jack realized, as he watched the carriage rattle down the drive and then vanish into the street. What would he do if Beryl saw him? Could he bear to look into her eyes after all this time? Perhaps she didn't remember him anymore. He wouldn't blame her for pretending he had never existed.

Yet in that moment, none of that mattered. He skipped back to the stables like a little child, whistling with joy. Beryl was alive and well. He laughed and prayed a silent hallelujah; the Lord had sent him here for a reason after all.

Part Six

Chapter Fourteen

One Year Later

Despite the calluses on Jack's hands, his palms ached fiercely as he swung the feed room door shut and bolted it. Crickets chirped in the cool night; it wouldn't be long before the first frost came and they were all gone. The stars were distant pinpricks above the dark stable yard as Jack swung his lantern around, checking over the horses one more time. Most were hidden in their loose boxes, champing on their hay.

"Goodnight, everyone," he called softly.

Distantly, a church bell rang as Jack made his way to the cottage door where Silas lived. He counted its tolls: ten long rings. He'd been working for sixteen hours, and exhaustion dragged at his limbs and the corners of his eyes.

As always, the church bell made him miss St. Luke's and Mrs. Brownstone and Reverend Samuel.

He expected to find a plate waiting for him at the cottage's back door. Instead, the lights still shone inside. Jack pushed the door open and nervously made his way into the kitchen.

"What are you doing here, boy?" Silas barked.

Jack jumped. He'd expected the old man to be abed already, but instead Silas sat by the kitchen fire, moodily rubbing his hip the way he did when Jack was going to have a terrible day.

"Just thought I'd see if the cook sent supper down, sir," he said.

Silas scoffed. "I told you I'd leave it on the doorstep, you stupid boy. What hour is this to come barging into a man's home?"

Jack refrained from reminding him that the cottage was meant to be his home, too. "Sorry, sir," he said instead.

"It's on the table." Silas nodded. "Take it and go. And I want to see you in the stables at dawn tomorrow, do you understand? Those horses have to be fed well before the young master takes that chestnut nag out hunting."

"Yes, sir," said Jack.

He grasped the plate on the kitchen table, wincing at the sight. The cook was nothing if not generous with the servants' meals, but Jack had the feeling that the meal she sent out was seldom the one that reached his hands. The food on the plate tonight was half a baked potato, a cold beet, and a few thin slices of chicken. Smears on the plate suggested that there had been gravy once. This was no longer the case.

He struggled with the temptation to cast a baleful glare at Silas, but crushed it. "Goodnight, sir," he said. Silas only grunted in reply as Jack left the cottage and made for the steps that led up to the loft over the horses' stables on the right.

Though without the warmth of a fire, the loft wasn't so bad. Jack had bought himself as many blankets as he needed; the housekeeper dispensed the wages herself and Silas couldn't interfere with those. The horses' bodies sent warmth to the loft, too, and his bed was a comfortable pile of hay.

Jack perched on the hay pile and munched his cold, insufficient dinner. The lantern hanging over his head swayed slightly as wind howled around the stables. Tomorrow would be cold; today had been wet. He hoped that the ground wouldn't freeze too hard for the hunting. Many hunters wouldn't ride on frozen ground for fear of breaking their horses' legs, but the young master had no such reservations.

Feeling suddenly very alone, Jack opened the small wooden box by his hay pile and unfolded the note he'd read a dozen times since receiving it last week. Reading the words was laborious work, but he could understand them well enough.

My dearest Jack,

It greatly pleases me to hear that you have been working with such faithfulness and diligence despite the poor attitude of your stablemaster. I trust that it will not be long before you may enjoy the benefits of your hard work.

We baptized a baby girl in the congregation yesterday— Amelia Caroline Shaw. Isn't that a beautiful name? I hope you can meet her when you have the funds to visit once again. Mrs. Brownstone and I miss you greatly.

Have you spoken with Beryl yet? I understand that she is difficult to reach in her position as the young lady's companion, but there must be a time that you may run into her without any impropriety. Jack, the Lord led you back to her. He didn't do so simply for you to ignore her. He goes with you. Do not be afraid!

With all of our love,

Samuel and Mrs. Brownstone.

Jack smiled as he folded the letter and tucked it into the box. Every night he told himself that he would compose a reply, but forming the letters was hard work, and his hands were exhausted. He would write back on Sunday, then.

Jack lay down and pillowed his head on the hay, thinking of the end of Samuel's letter. *Beryl*. She was peerlessly beautiful, and from the laugh he occasionally heard from the house's high windows, as wonderful and kind as ever. Perhaps Samuel was right. Perhaps he should pluck up the courage to speak with her...

Exhaustion wrapped him in its warm embrace before he could complete the thought.

"Steady, Becky!" Jack soothed the little black pony as he pulled the soft brush through her mane. "It's all right."

Becky flared her nostrils. She was a hasty little animal, with a refined head and high-set tail that suggested she was far more than the average Scottish or moorland pony. The housekeeper had said that Becky belonged to Annabel, yet Jack had never saddled her except to ride out himself for exercise. She was a fiery beast who'd thrown Jack more than once as he fumbled to learn riding, but he liked her. Rumour had it that Annabel was never well enough to go outside. Perhaps that was why Jack hardly ever saw her—and why the pony stood endlessly in her box.

"We'll ride later," he promised, smoothing Becky's mane.

The little creature snorted as if with disgust, then suddenly shied, pulling back against her headcollar. Jack gripped the lead rein and looked around, startled, for whatever danger had spooked her. Running feet echoed outside. He heard raised voices, then shouting.

"What's going on?" he called, popping his head over the door as a scullery-maid sprinted past.

"The young master's fallen from his horse!" she cried. "It's all very exciting!"

Jack's heart froze as he glanced toward the empty box belonging to the beautiful chestnut gelding, Warrior. A fall! Just as he'd feared on this frozen ground.

He loosed the pony and rushed into the stable yard, then followed the scampering scullery-maid around the stables to the front drive. A small crowd had already gathered at the steps as curious servants gaped something.

Jack glimpsed the flash of a chestnut coat through the crowd and pushed his way to the front, and his heart stopped.

The young master strode beside Warrior, his hat gone, his hair in disarray. Mud smeared one side of his body and blood marred his smooth cheek where something had lightly scratched him. There was an ugly bruise on his jaw, and he swung his riding crop in his hand as he marched toward the house. For once, Warrior did not prance beside his rider. Instead, he moved slowly, ears tipped back, resisting the pressure on the reins as the young master dragged him along. The big animal barely dotted his left front hoof on the ground with each step. Ugly swelling marred the smooth tendons below the large joint.

"Stupid beast!" the young master burst out.

The servants shuffled aside, jostling Jack, as Mr. Ashcroft rushed down the steps. "Sebastian, my boy, whatever happened? Are you hurt?"

"This beast refused a fence, Papa!" said the young master petulantly. "You said he was the bravest, fastest hunter you've ever seen, but he refused and refused until I made him go, and then the ungrateful creature fell on the other side. I landed in the ditch!"

The ditch! Jack wanted to cry out in Warrior's defence. No wonder the intelligent animal had refused to jump; he must have seen the dark ice on the other side.

"Are you hurt?" said Mr. Ashcroft again.

"I'm cold and soaked, and all my friends watched," said the young master.

"Then you're not hurt," Mr. Ashcroft barked, "and you ruined this good, bold horse for nothing!"

Everyone jumped at his harsh tone. Jack gaped; he hadn't expected this of the master of the house.

"I told you—" the young master began.

"Go inside," said Mr. Ashcroft. "I will deal with you later. Now, where on earth is Mr. Thorne?"

"I'm here, sir!" Silas wheezed, limping up to them. "I'm here!" He seized Warrior's reins as the young master stormed to the house. "I heard what happened. Right pity, it is."

"Pity!" said Mr. Ashcroft. "I would think the amount of money I paid for this animal would constitute rather more than a pity. What do you say, Mr. Thorne? Will he be sound again?"

Silas drove his hard, knobby fingers into the delicate limb. "He's done for, sir. I'll send for the knacker."

"No!" Jack burst out.

Everyone turned to stare at him, especially Silas, whose sneer grew uglier than ever.

"Silence, boy," he barked. "What are you doing here? Go back to the stable."

"Please," said Jack. "I'm sorry, I don't mean to be defiant, but Warrior might not need to go to the knacker."

"Boy—" Silas began.

"Quiet," said Mr. Ashcroft. "Let him speak."

Jack's heart thudded. He shuffled forward and stroked Warrior's forehead. "Sir, the farrier told me of a horse that tore his tendons and healed at the Burlington's' manor. He even raced again. It took time, but he got well. Maybe Warrior can get well too, sir."

"I remember that," Mr. Ashcroft murmured. "I backed that horse afterward and he won at Ascot."

"I'll do anything, sir," said Jack. "I'll bandage his leg and rub it with liniment and stand him in the pond. Let me try, sir. Please," he begged.

"How dare you speak to the master, you wretch?" Silas cried.

"Leave the boy alone, Silas. He's been more helpful than you," said Mr. Ashcroft. "This horse was expensive and I have no desire to lose him. Go ahead, boy. Do what you can." He patted Warrior's neck. "Perhaps you will both surprise me."

He turned away, and the housekeeper came bustling out, appalled. "Back to work!" she ordered. "All of you!"

Silas gave him a long glare. "When the knacker comes for that horse, boy," he hissed, "you'll be sorry." Then he stormed away.

Jack was the last to leave. He moved slowly and gently as Warrior hobbled beside him back toward the box, stroking the wounded creature and speaking gently. And unbeknownst to him, a small figure with flaming red hair watched from the window, her jewel-blue eyes filling with tears.

Jack slowly unwound the bandage from Warrior's leg and smiled. He gripped a hard brush and removed the clay poultice that clung to the chestnut hair, then moved his hands gently up and down the leg, feeling for swelling.

"Good boy." Jack grinned as he patted Warrior's shoulder. "Good boy!"

The big horse turned his head from his hayrack and huffed his sweet breath in Jack's face as if to say thank you, then returned to his meal.

Beaming, Jack took a currycomb and brush from their place in the wall and worked on Warrior's coat, polishing it to a fine shine. Should the master glimpse him leading Warrior down to the stream to cool his legs in the icy water, he would see an animal glowing with health, not the crippled beast that Silas constantly suggested Warrior really was. The truth was, after two weeks of treatment, the big animal could walk easily once more. He would get better, Jack believed. He thanked God in his thoughts for it.

"You'll get better, old boy," he said, working the brush over the satiny red coat. "You'll be well and strong again soon. Who knows if the young master will ever want to ride you again? Maybe he won't be given a choice. Either way, you'll be alive, old fellow, and I'll be glad that—"

Warrior raised his head and emitted a sudden snort, then a deep nicker, a sound of welcome. He moved to the front of his box and put his head over the door as if seeing someone he liked.

Jack frowned, puzzled. He'd never seen Warrior react to anyone except himself that way. He peered over the door, and his world froze and shrank to this one crystalline moment.

Beryl was right there, in the flesh, alive and smiling, mere feet away from him.

Jack's heart felt as though it grew wings and turned leaden all at once. Excitement and terror drenched his body in cold fire. Beryl stood a few feet from the box, her eyes fixed on his face, a basket of carrots on her arm. She wore a lovely blue cotton dress that brought out the colour of her eyes and her hair was tied up in a bright ribbon. Jack realized he had never seen her up close while she was well and healthy before, and she was even more of a vision than his memory suggested. She was perfect.

For a moment, he thought wildly that he could still hide from her. Then she said, "Hello, Jackie."

Surprise and delight washed over him. Jack's knees buckled. He had to grab the door to keep from falling over.

"You remember me," he blurted out.

Her laugh was like the soft trill of a bluebird. "Of course I remember you. You were my only friend."

"Your only friend!" Tears filled Jack's eyes. "And I betrayed you."

Beryl's lips parted, but she said nothing.

Jack wanted to run and hide in the loft, to never face this moment that he had both longed for and dreaded for the better part of his life. Instead, he prayed for strength, and somehow it flooded him. He stepped from the stable and shut the door behind him, then turned to Beryl and met her eyes.

"I'm so sorry, Beryl," he said. The words were bitter on his tongue, but when he'd spoken them, a tremendous weight lifted from his shoulders. "I betrayed you and abandoned you. I left you in your worst need, and I said horrible, hurtful things to you. I'm so sorry. I should have done better."

Beryl blinked, then blinked again, but couldn't stop the tears from flooding her eyes. "I thought there was something wrong with me," she whispered, "and that that was why you left."

Her words tore him. His fears were true; what he'd done had festered within her, had plagued her. Jack couldn't stop his own tears from flowing.

"There was never anything wrong with you," he cried. "It was all my fault, Beryl. Please… please… know how sorry I am. I should never have done it, and I'm so sorry." He gulped at his tears. "Can you forgive me?"

Beryl stared at him, her eyes suddenly shining. "Oh, Jack. You were just a scared little boy. Of course I forgive you." She edged nearer to him, then held out her hands. "I forgive you!"

The words fell on his soul like sunlight thawing frozen ground. Jack took her hands in his, bowed his head, and allowed himself to weep as he praised God in his heart.

"I can hardly believe it's really you," Beryl whispered. "I saw you so many times at the workhouse, hanging about at the palisades, but every time I ran to you, you ran off."

"I was scared," said Jack. "I didn't know how to face what I'd done to you. But what happened? One day I went to the workhouse and you were gone."

"I came here," said Beryl. "Annabel was dying and she wouldn't let anyone come near her, no one at all. The doctor said she needed a companion in a hurry, a girl who could make her happy again and be her friend, and there was no time to look for anyone else. The Ashcroft's had me brought from the workhouse and made presentable, and then I went to be Annabel's companion, and we were friends at once. I know she's rich, but she's lovely, Jack, so lovely. She got better at once. She was so terribly lonely and tired of all the adults fussing over her."

"You saved her," said Jack.

Beryl laughed and shook her head. "Not like you saved *him*!" She nodded at the hunter. "I saw you from the windows a few times, and I thought it looked like you, but I couldn't be sure… not until you spoke up so boldly to Mr. Ashcroft and saved this horse's life. I knew it was you then. And I—" She paused. "I thought perhaps you'd come to me, that you'd seen me at last. But then I realized that you wouldn't come. Annabel said not to talk to you, that you didn't remember me, and she didn't want me to get my heart broken. But you do remember. It really was you all those years."

"I always longed to find you." Jack's throat knotted. "But in the end, it seems it was you who came to find me."

"Oh, Jack!" said Beryl.

Her small hands quivered in his. Though, at fifteen, Jack did not yet have the words to convey what he felt, he would later look back at that moment as the one in which he fell hopelessly in love.

Summer was verdant on the beautifully tended lawns bordering Ashcroft Manor. Jack straightened his cap as he strode up the drive with a spring in his step, wearing new shirt and trousers freshly made for him thanks to his increase in wages. He held Warrior's lead rein in one hand as the mighty animal bounded and bucked beside him, his coat flashing like copper in the sun. Four strong legs bore the saddled and bridled horse boldly to the bottom of the steps.

The young master waited at the top of the steps, his lip twisted in distaste, but he dared not say anything with the iron hand of his father on his shoulder.

"Now don't be a fool with this expensive animal this time," Mr. Ashcroft growled.

"Why's the groom bringing him out for me?" the young master demanded. "It should be the stablemaster. How dare you treat me like some commoner, boy!" he yelled at Jack.

Mr. Ashcroft's hand tightened. "Young Mr. Finch is the reason that several hundred pounds' worth of horseflesh is still alive. Besides, here comes Mr. Thorne with my horse."

Silas shuffled up the drive, sneering, as he dragged Mr. Ashcroft's hunter by the reins.

The big black animal was utterly docile but rolled his eyes in wariness as Silas yanked him to a halt.

The young master slouched down the steps, took the reins, and scrambled gracelessly into the saddle. He wheeled Warrior around and set off down the drive at a bold canter. Jack felt a grin spread over his face as he watched the mighty animal move with strong, springy steps, sound as ever.

Mr. Ashcroft mounted with a sigh. As Silas released his horse's head, he looked down at Jack. "You have done us a service, young man."

"It was my pleasure, sir." Jack touched his forelock.

"I can tell that seeing Warrior well again is reward enough for you, but it's good news that your increased wage has reached you." Mr. Ashcroft glanced severely at Silas, then spurred his horse to canter after his wayward son.

"Fool," Silas muttered. "You should've let me shoot that animal. Its leg will give way while the young master rides and get them both killed. Then who will be the master's little hero?"

Jack merely smiled.

"What are you so happy about?" Silas demanded. He cuffed Jack sharply on the back of the head. "Get back to work!"

Jack strode off, muffling his laughter. It was nearly absurd that Silas thought he could stem Jack's happiness.

After all, tomorrow was Sunday. The afternoon was all his.

The vegetable garden smelled of damp earth, ripening tomatoes, and the sweet kiss of strawberries warming in the sun. It had none of the flower garden's splendour as Beryl described it from Annabel's regular little walks in the sunshine, but to Jack, no place could be more beautiful.

He sat cross-legged on the cool earth, admiring a butterfly that dipped and bobbed amid pumpkin flowers. Beside him, Beryl stretched out on a patch of grass with her hands behind her head. Annabel's governess perched on a stool nearby, reading, and paid them no attention.

"Isn't it a lovely day?" said Beryl. "I could soak in this sunshine for hours."

"It's wonderful," Jack agreed.

"I've seen nicer weather in only one place—Spain. We went on holiday there once, when Annabel was still strong enough to travel. She refused to go without me." Beryl laughed. "The people and the food are awfully strange, but I did like going to the beach. The water was very nice. I could put my toes in it."

"The beach," said Jack. "I don't think I've ever seen the beach. The docks, perhaps. But I don't think it's the same thing."

"Not at all," said Beryl, smiling.

Jack closed his eyes, enjoying the sunlight. "Maybe we'll go to Spain one day when I'm a stablemaster. I'll have a whole yard full of those big white Spanish horses that can dance."

"Dancing horses! I think you've gone mad," said Beryl.

"We'll have a cottage by the sea," said Jack, "and gather seashells every day and fish for our suppers."

Beryl laughed. "That sounds lovely, but we had other plans, remember?"

Jack opened his eyes to take in her teasing smile. "Other plans?"

"Yes. We were going to find your mama and live on a farm in the countryside," said Beryl.

Jack suddenly remembered their whispered daydreams among the soot sacks. He bowed his head, longing piercing him.

"You've had no news of her, then," said Beryl softly.

Jack shook his head. "None. I don't even know her name, Beryl. There's no way to find her." He paused, then smiled. "But I used to believe I would never find you, either, and here we are. It's like a miracle."

Beryl glanced at the governess, then placed her hand over his. "I think so too."

Jack's pen scratched painstakingly over the paper as he bent over a box in the loft. It was a lumpy surface, and the letters he formed were messy, but he knew Samuel wouldn't mind. Ever since he'd gotten an extra sixpence each week, he was able to write to Samuel once a week instead of once a month, and his writing was getting better as a result.

Dear Reverend Samuel and Mrs. Brownstone,

I'm still so happy about Beryl. It's truly seems a miracle. We visit together every Sunday afternoon when we have time off.

Having Beryl with me makes me want to dream, like you said. I never thought I could have a future. But one day I want to be a stablemaster.

Jack paused, nibbling on the end of his pen, but decided not to add that he would be a far kinder stablemaster than Silas Thorne. Reverend Samuel didn't need to know how cruel and wicked Silas was; Jack knew it would torture the vicar to know how Jack was being treated. There was, after all, nothing Samuel could do about it anymore. There were two other children living in the vicarage now, urchins he'd rescued the same as he did with Jack.

When I'm a stablemaster, he added, *I want to marry Beryl.*

The words spilled from his pen almost before he could think about them. A pulse of wild delight ran through him at the thought. Married to Beryl! It was beyond his wildest dreams to have a wife so pretty and sweet and kind as Beryl. But she was here now, and she liked him. She was everything to him.

He hummed as he finished the rest of the letter.

We need to be older, I know. But I love her. I know I do.

Let me know how Mrs. Jones is.

Love,

Jack.

Chapter Fifteen

Percy kept his hand securely wrapped around Mabel's as they sat in Nathan Goulding's office. Though an open window admitted the warm air of summer, Mabel had felt as though a cold wind was blowing through her from the moment she'd stepped through the door and seen the look on Nathan's face.

The investigator seemed to be struggling to find words now. He sat behind the desk, his fingertips pressed together, his eyes resting on the desk instead of focusing on Mabel and Percy.

"Please, Mr. Goulding." Mabel cleared her throat. "Your letter said there was progress at last with finding my Jack."

It had been another long, cold, terrifying year without any news from Nathan Goulding other than that he was chasing down lead after unfruitful lead. Ugly doubts had begun to arise in Mabel as a result.

But now, the furrow in his brow woke something in her that was uglier still: a terrible fear that he'd found Jack, and yet she would still never hold her firstborn in her arms again.

"There has been great progress, yes." Nathan looked up and exhaled. "That's the good news."

Mabel stiffened. Percy's hand tightened on hers.

He asked the question she was too afraid to voice. "What's the bad news, then, Mr. Goulding?" Nathan took a deep breath. "I'm afraid it's the worst kind of news. It appears that Jack was indeed involved with a gang of child thieves. The rumours we heard turned out to be true."

Mabel gasped, her hand flying to her mouth. "Oh no! What's happened to him? What's happened to my Little Jack?"

Nathan continued gently, "After much searching, and thanks to an arrest record and a witness statement, I was able to confirm the leader of the gang Jack was involved with." Mabel's head snapped up. "Who is he?"

"She," said Nathan. "A girl named Elizabeth Addleby."

"A girl," said Mabel faintly. Perhaps a girl would have been kinder to her Jack-Jack than a boy.

"With her name, I was able to find out more about her," said Nathan. "It seems that she was born in a workhouse to an impoverished mother whose name is not recorded and who died in childbirth, hence the strange surname. She escaped when she was seven years old and survived on the streets. When I asked people in the area about 'Liz Addleby,' they could tell me that she and her gang of friends were a menace to society. Many saw a boy several years younger than her running with her." Nathan paused. "There is no doubt that Jack was with the gang for several years."

"*Was* with the gang?" Mabel croaked.

Nathan shook his head. "He is no longer with them."

"How can you be sure? Have you gone to speak with them?" said Mabel.

Nathan hesitated. "I can't, Mrs. Mitchell. The gang no longer exists."

Mabel's heart froze. Her hand trembled in Percy's.

"A policeman of the area was able to tell me what happened." Nathan painfully paused. "Elizabeth Addleby was crushed under the wheels of a carriage while fleeing from a shop she'd robbed.

When the policeman arrived, three younger children were trying to revive her, but she was beyond human aid. She perished on impact. The policeman captured the three little children and knew of a fourth boy, one they called Finn, who escaped. No one in the area has seen him since."

"And Jack?" Mabel croaked. "What about my Jack?"

"I'm sorry, Mrs. Mitchell. I don't know yet what happened to him after that," said Nathan. "He was not among the children that were captured with Elizabeth's body. Nor do any witnesses remember seeing him flee the scene. Indeed, several said they hadn't seen him with the gang for months before it happened."

Mabel squeezed her eyes tightly shut. All she could think of was her little boy, her Jack-Jack, succumbing to the same fate as poor young Elizabeth, who had never had any chance in this world. How many dangers did a young thief face every day? Speeding carriages, savage dogs, angry shopkeepers with blunderbusses— had her baby ended up as a floating corpse in the river?

A small sob choked her. She covered her face with her hands.

"He may yet be out there, Mrs. Mitchell," said Nathan. "He must be somewhere. I promise you, I will find him."

Mae could say nothing. It was Percy who thanked the investigator and helped her to her feet, then guided her from his office while she sobbed into her handkerchief. She could summon no courage, nor any resolve; only a heartfelt, broken prayer.

Oh, Lord, help my boy, help my boy, help my boy!

The crash of thunder jerked Jack from his sleep. He sat up with a gasp as lightning bathed his world in shocking white. Panic clutched his chest for a moment before he realized that it was only a storm. The thunder rolled again, and the steady tumult of rain drummed on the stable roof mere feet above Jack's head.

Jack relaxed onto his bed of hay, wiping a sweat of fright from his face. The storm droned around him, but he heard no stamping of hooves in the boxes below. Sometimes Warrior could grow skittish in storms. Tonight, though, the fine animal was quiet. All was well.

Jack pulled his covers up to his shoulder and closed his eyes, thinking of how beautiful the clean-washed world would become morning, with the horse paddocks more verdantly green than before and the horses frisking and bucking over the rich grass in the morning...

The thump of hoofbeats yanked him from the edge of sleep. He sat up with a gasp as Warrior stamped and snorted in his stable, but it wasn't the storm that startled him. The next flash of lightning illuminated a hunched figure crouching in the doorway to the loft.

Jack's heart jumped into his throat. He flew to his feet.

"It's me, boy," Silas barked. "Wake up! How can you sleep through all this? I've been shouting your name all the way across the yard!"

Jack blinked, startled. He'd never seen Silas up at this hour, let alone in the rain.

"M-Mr. Thorne?" he stammered. "What's wrong?"

"Saddle the young master's horse at once," Silas barked, then turned to stump away.

Jack scrambled after him. "Warrior! Why? Why could the young master want to ride out on a night like this? It's too dangerous!"

"Stop asking questions and do it, boy!" Silas screamed.

He raised his hand, and Jack cowered, terrified of a blow. But this time, his fear was satisfactory. Silas sneered and limped away.

With pounding heart, Jack scrambled to the bottom of the stairs and ran to the tack room through the deluge. Lightning tore the sky, and Warrior gave a high-pitched whinny as Jack jogged across the wet yard, saddle on his arm, bridle over his shoulder. He couldn't fathom why the young master would ride at a time like this, but supposed that it wasn't true. Silas simply wanted to chase Jack around in the dark and teach him a lesson. It wasn't unusual.

All the same, if he didn't saddle the horse, Silas would make life worse for them both.

Jack slipped into the stable. The wide-eyed, worried animal calmed instantly and rested his big head on Jack's shoulder.

"Good boy," said Jack. "It's all right."

He raised the saddle onto Warrior's smooth chestnut back and loosely buckled the girth, then eased the leather of the bridle over his silken ears. Warrior took the bit as though it were a carrot. He lowered his head patiently as Jack made all the small, gentle motions of ensuring the bridle was comfortable: smoothing the mane beneath the headpiece, tucking the forelock over the browband, securing noseband and throat lash just tight enough.

Finally, Jack tightened the girth and led the big horse into the rain. Warrior flattened his ears in protest but did not resist as Jack jogged across the yard. Hooves slapped in the puddles as they trotted together to the front door, and with a ripple of shock, Jack saw that Silas was right. The main doors stood open, and four silhouettes stood on the steps against its golden light. Fear speared through Jack as he recognized Beryl.

He wanted to cry out to her, but he kept his head down and ran to the bottom of the steps instead.

"Listen to me, my boy." Mr. Ashcroft's voice trembled as he addressed his son with a hand on his shoulder. "You must ride now as you have never ridden in your life. Your sister's life depends on it. Do you understand? You must go for the doctor with all the speed God has given that magnificent animal, or our dear Annabel will be lost to the world."

A sob tore from Beryl's lips. Tears streaked her face, and she pressed her fingertips to her lips, shaking from head to toe.

For once, the young master's face was solemn. "Yes, Father. I understand."

"Please," Mrs. Ashcroft sobbed.

"Good." Mr. Ashcroft shook his head. "If it were not for my hand..." He'd broken it in a shooting accident the day before.

"I'll do it, Father. I will," said the young master, "and you know Warrior is the fastest horse in the stable in any case."

"Go," said Mr. Ashcroft.

The young master ran down the stairs. Jack ran down the stirrups, aware of Warrior's quivering tension as the majestic, frightened beast stood beside him.

"You have to be good now, old boy," he whispered, stroking Warrior's nose. "Annabel needs you."

The horse stared at him out of liquid, uncomprehending eyes.

"Give him to me!" the young master barked, snatching the reins.

Warrior snorted and reared, front hooves flailing.

"Stop that!" The young master yanked the reins, and Warrior landed briefly on all fours. With a great heavy pull, the boy hoisted himself into the saddle and jerked Warrior's head around. He slammed his spurs into the horse's flanks with no regard, and Warrior lurched forward at a dead gallop, slipping and snorting as he charged down the drive.

Jack clasped his hands over his chest, terror and hope colliding within him. *Go, boy!* he silently urged the big horse.

They were not yet a hundred yards down the gravel when disaster struck. A jagged bolt of lightning tore across the sky, its flash blinding to both man and beast. Warrior's snort was one of pure terror. He bounded to a halt, jolting his rider in the saddle, and froze where he stood.

"Go on, you lazy beast!" the young master cried, and lashed his whip across the horse's ribs.

Warrior knew only pain and fear. He sprang into the air, ripping his head down, and kicked out sideways. Few riders could have stayed on; the young master was not one of them. He landed on the gravel, rolling, and Warrior spun and bolted back to Jack with his tail high and eyes wild.

"Whoa, boy!" Jack cried, dismay curdling in his belly. "Whoa!"

The young master was on his feet almost before anyone could be frightened, unhurt, but irate. He stormed toward the house as Jack lunged for Warrior's reins and brought the panicking horse to a steaming, snorting halt. Mr. Ashcroft was suddenly beside him, his face a grey, distraught mask.

"Give him to me!" the young master snapped as he strode up to Jack.

"No," barked Mr. Ashcroft.

"What? Why not?" the young master demanded in a fine temper.

"Because I already stand to lose one child tonight," said Mr. Ashcroft. "You'll not remount this animal, not in this weather. I won't lose both of you."

His words slammed like a coffin lid. The young master's face drained of all colour; it was as though this night had been a high adventure to him, but reality struck him at that moment.

A terrible scream of mourning rent the night. "No!" Beryl wailed. "Nooooo!"

She collapsed to her knees at the top of the steps, her hands covering her face, sobbing. Mrs. Ashcroft pressed a pale and trembling hand to her mouth as tears streamed over her cheeks.

Beryl's pain cut through Jack like a knife. Perhaps driven by it, the words came out before he could stop them.

"I'll go, sir," he said.

"What?" said Mr. Ashcroft.

The young master gave a harsh laugh. "You? You're no rider."

"I've ridden him out plenty of times for exercise," said Jack. "He'll go for me, sir. He trusts me. We can get the doctor." He stared up at Mr. Ashcroft with all the boldness he could muster. "I know we can."

Mr. Ashcroft stared.

"Why, you—" the young master began.

"Anything for Annabel," said Mr. Ashcroft. "Go, boy, and may all God's angels ride with you."

Jack's heart thudded. Beryl stared at him, her hands in her lap now, terror filling her eyes. He longed to wrap her in his arms. Instead, he did the only thing he could for her: he grasped the reins, thrust a foot into the stirrup, and sprang up into Warrior's saddle. The big animal stood motionless and trembling as he found the other stirrup while lightning crashed around them.

Jack leaned closer. "We must do this for Annabel, my boy," he said, "and for Beryl. Please. We have to do this."

Warrior's ear flicked back to catch his voice, and the horse's body tensed. Jack offered up a silent prayer of hope and squeezed Warrior's sides with his calves. The big animal moved forward at a brisk trot, his mouth tense on the reins, his movement jarring with fear, but willing.

When they reached the bottom of the hill, Jack nudged him into a canter and they flowed out of the gate and down the street. A left turn, a right turn, and then they were on the main road to the doctor's house. Thunder and lightning crashed and flickered all around them, but for Jack only the sound of Warrior's hoofbeats and the huff of his breathing between his knees existed.

It seemed that, for Warrior, only the guiding hand on his reins and the gentle words of his rider existed, for the big animal took not one misstep. Jack knew the road to the doctor—he passed by that house on his way to the tram back to St. Luke's—but he knew it as one that took an hour to traverse. On Warrior, the time flashed by in minutes. With Jack crouching over the horse's mane, he urged him to a full gallop, hooves ringing on the road, and they sailed across the distance with all the speed in the world.

Sooner than he'd dreamed, Jack saw it: the doctor's tall white house looming in the night. But the gates were shut. Ignoring every rule he knew, Jack swung Warrior around and kicked him toward the wall surrounding the doctor's garden. With a grunt of effort, Warrior flung himself into the air. They flew together for a breathless moment, and then landed on the grass and galloped up to the main entrance.

A great brass bell hung before the door there for summoning the man of medicine. Jack threw himself from the saddle and clung to the reins with one hand as he frantically rang the bell with the other.

Footsteps sounded within the house. It seemed to take an eternity for them to reach the door, which opened to reveal a whiskery man in a robe.

"Dr. Whitmore!" Jack cried. "Please, you must come quickly. It's Annabel."

"You're from Ashcroft Manor?" said Dr. Whitmore.

"Yes, sir. Please hurry. She's in a bad way," said Jack.

The doctor peered at the storm outside, but it seemed to be passing. The lightning came less frequently now; the rain was a drizzle instead of a deluge.

"I will bring my carriage around at once," said Dr. Whitmore. "Ride ahead of us, boy, or the carriage-horses might be frightened of the weather; it seems yours is not."

A few minutes later, they set off into the rain once more, Warrior briskly trotting, the carriage clattering as they struggled to keep up.

The rain had nearly stopped when they reached Ashcroft Manor once more. Dr. Whitmore drove straight to the front door, but Jack turned Warrior's weary head for the stables and rode him quietly into the yard.

Warrior was hot and sweaty but not blowing when they reached the stables. There was no sign of Silas, but Jack relished the peace as he led Warrior inside and rubbed him down, then spread a blanket over him with straw underneath it to dry him off. He was feeding the big animal a warm mash when a tremulous little voice spoke from the yard.

"J-Jackie?"

Jack looked up. Beryl stood in the drizzle, her red hair dark and flat with water, her eyes filled with tears.

"Oh, Beryl!" Jack let himself out of the stable. "You mustn't stand in the rain. You'll catch your death." He grasped a horse rug and wrapped it around her shoulders, then led her into the shelter of the feed room.

Beryl sat on a sack of oats and sobbed, trembling and miserable, dripping on the floor. Jack could think of nothing to do except to sit beside her with an arm around her shoulders.

"I don't know what's going to happen," Beryl sobbed. "She's so ill, Jackie. She's so very ill. I can't bear to lose her, I can't."

"It'll be all right," said Jack softly. "We can only pray for her now."

As they prayed together, a small, selfish thought crept into the back of Jack's mind. If Annabel died, what would happen to Beryl?

Would he ever see her again?

Chapter Sixteen

Jack cast another longing glance up at the manor house as he plodded across the stable yard, laden by a bucket of water. Three long days had passed since his ride in the storm. Warrior's leg had remained cool and tight, with no sign of swelling. But it was small consolation in the face of complete silence from the manor house. None of the Ashcrofts had called for horses or carriages to go out. Jack could only guess at their reasons for being cloistered in there.

"Oi!" Silas barked. "What are you dawdling about for, boy? Hurry up and get the watering done!"

"Yes, sir," said Jack.

He hastened to Storm's stable and set the water bucket inside. The big animal shook his ears, uneasy at Jack's tension, and dipped his nose into the bucket.

Jack shut the door and crossed the yard again, aware of Silas's baleful eye as the old man sat outside, mending a broken piece of harness for which he'd blamed Jack. He fetched another empty bucket from the pony's stall and kept his head down as he hurried out of the yard and out of Silas's sight to fill the bucket by the pump at the back of the stables.

He'd no sooner set the bucket beneath the pump when a small figure shuffled from the hedge nearby, and his hand froze on the handle in shock and delight.

"Beryl!" Jack cried.

She gave him a tentative smile that lifted his head. Beryl's cheeks were pinched and pale, but her eyes shone as she hurried to him, hands outstretched.

"Oh, Jack," she cried, "it's marvellous, it's just marvellous!"

"What is it?" said Jack, grasping her hands.

She laughed, joyous tears flowing over her cheeks. "She's all right. Annabel's all right."

Relief made Jack's shoulders sag. "Oh, Beryl, I'm so glad."

"It was so frightening, Jack. I didn't know if she could live. She was so very ill... But the fever's finally left her, and Dr. Whitmore came by again this morning. He says that the worst is over. She's weak, but she'll get better," said Beryl.

"I'm sure it's all thanks to your nursing," said Jack.

Beryl laughed. "It's all thanks to God and you know it." She paused, her smile fading. "But Jackie... there's something else."

Jack's heart stuttered. "What?"

Sudden tears filled Beryl's eyes. She looked away, and for a few interminable moments, she couldn't speak.

"What is it, Beryl?" Jack asked softly. "You know you can tell me."

"It's consumption, Jackie," said Beryl. Her voice broke. "The doctor... he says it'll never really go away. She can't live in London anymore. The air is too dirty here; it'll kill her."

Jack's heart turned into a block of ice in his chest. "What does that mean?" he croaked.

"It means that Annabel's moving to the seaside. There's a town not far from London, right in the country, where the air is clear and everything is lovely. Annabel's so excited. It's so beautiful there, but—" Beryl swallowed. "She's asked me to go with her. It's the only thing I can do."

Understanding flooded Jack at once, but at the same time, it felt as though something had just kicked him in the belly. The air left his lungs; pain blossomed through him and for a long time, he couldn't quite speak.

"I don't want to leave you," said Beryl, mistaking his silence for anger. "I really don't. I want to stay here. But I don't have a choice, Jackie." She was nearly crying now. "Annabel doesn't have anyone else she trusts like she trusts me. I can't leave her now, either, and… and where would I go? Where would I work?"

"Beryl, it's all right," said Jack softly. "I understand."

Beryl swallowed. "You do?"

"Yes," said Jack. He fought for control over his voice. "You can't leave a friend when they're so unwell. I would never ask you to stay for my sake."

Beryl's shoulders sagged, but her eyes were still filled with tears as they searched his face. "Oh, Jack, I'll miss you so much."

"I'll miss you, too," Jack murmured, "but I'll write all the time. I promise."

She brightened slightly. "I'll write, too. Annabel taught me years ago. And the Ashcrofts will visit Annabel from time to time. Maybe they'll ask you to come with them to look after the horses."

Jack supposed the chances were slim, but he clung onto that fragment of hope as the world seemed to be crumpling around him.

The day of the great parting was grey and raining, and Jack was not allowed to wrap Beryl in his arms. He was, in fact, not even allowed to speak to her; the occasion was reserved for the Ashcrofts as Annabel wept on her mother's neck and Mr. Ashcroft made a stern face over his sorrow.

All that Jack could do was to watch as the footmen loaded Beryl's things into the carriage alongside Annabel's. He stood at Storm's head, holding him, while Annabel clambered into the carriage.

Beryl left the manor house last. She wore a dress the colour of her eyes, perfect, pale blue, and it ripple around her knees as she descended the stairs with more elegance than the noblest lady. She faced straight ahead, her expression carved of marble, but her lower lip delicately trembled as she walked.

At the moment when she reached the carriage, all of Jack's heart wanted to do one of two things: to run to her, or to look away. They'd said their tearful goodbyes that morning behind the stables, snatching a moment's privacy to cling to one another's hands, Beryl sobbing, Jack trying his best not to weep, to be strong for her. But now he wanted to rush to her and fling his arms around her and beg her to stay. Surely, surely, nothing was more important than being together.

Jack knew full well that they both had duties to tend to. It was for their sake that he said nothing, but it was for Beryl that he did not abandon her in that moment. He did not lift his eyes from her, and in the last second, he was rewarded. With her hand on the carriage door, beryl looked over at him, and her heart shone in those jewel-bright eyes.

Oh! Those eyes! Their lustre! He had looked into them every day since she discovered him, and how he longed for that privilege to remain forever!

But it did not. He could not force it. All he could do was to watch, helpless, as Beryl vanished into the carriage and the coachman snapped the whip. Then he released Storm's head and stepped back as the carriage rattled down the drive, taking his entire heart—his entire world—with it.

The sky was as grey and heavy as Jack's heart. Though the rain did not yet fall, the air was oppressive with its imminent coming. The pressure made the horses stamp and snort in their stables, making his life difficult as they trod on his feet and accidentally knocked into him while he hung their water buckets and checked their hay racks.

"Oi! You! Boy!" Silas barked.

Jack wondered wearily how long he'd have to work under the heartless stablemaster for his name to be remembered. Fleetingly, he wished to pretend he hadn't heard, and quietly stay in the pony's stable until the old man gave up searching. But that was not how Reverend Samuel had taught him to be.

He strode to the front of the box and forced a smile onto his face. "Yes, sir?"

"The young master and his father are back from their hack," Silas snapped. "Help me at once."

The old stablemaster set off toward the front of the manor, his limp worse than ever in this weather, and Jack tried his best to feel sorry for him as he followed.

Still, it was far easier to feel sorry for himself. Every time he was summoned to the front of the manor—which was increasingly often these days—he longed to see Beryl's face in the window or hear her laughter drifting through an open door.

Instead, there was only the lowering storm and the clatter of hooves as Mr. Ashcroft and the young master rode up the hill. Warrior led the way, rudely preceding Mr. Ashcroft's black horse by several hundred feet. He reached Jack with flaring nostrils and tossing head.

"What are you doing here?" the young master demanded, yanking the reins to make the splendid animal stand still.

Jack gritted his teeth against the frustration flaring in him. "I'm here to take your horse, sir."

"Well, you don't belong here. You should be on the muck heap," said the young master. "You're nothing but a scruffy stable hand." He wheeled Warrior around, sneering, and rode toward Silas instead.

Mr Ashcroft hadn't heard the exchange; he never did. "Ah, Jack," he said. "I'm pleased to see you." He gently reined in his horse as he reached Jack. "Are you well, boy?"

Jack glanced around, aware of Silas' jealous, irate eyes upon him.

"Yes, sir," he mumbled, not meeting Mr. Ashcroft's eyes. He reached for the horse's bridle.

"You're a shy one, aren't you?" said Mr. Ashcroft, dismounting. "You should know that I don't take it lightly that I owe you my daughter's life. Had you not ridden for the doctor…"

Jack stared at the ground, saying nothing. He wondered how it was possible that Mr. Ashcroft wasn't aware of the bitter hatred and jealousy pouring from Silas and the young master just a few feet away.

"Father, it's about to rain," said the young master petulantly. "Why are we standing around out here? We'll get as ill as Annabel."

Jack took the horse's reins and Mr. Ashcroft turned away, leaving him in Silas' sneering presence. He ducked his head and hastened to the stables, but he didn't move fast enough. Silas reached out and struck the back of his head with an iron hand, making Warrior snort in panic.

"Upstart," he hissed. "You'll taste my whip for your cheek."

Jack hung his head as he plodded to the stables. He knew it was true. The heavens opened a moment later, and he walked through the frigid, bucketing rain, Silas' curses and shouts following him all the way.

His heart throbbed with the loss of Beryl. The world was nothing but cold and emptiness now. He longed to leave this all behind, to scream at Silas, to tell Mr. Ashcroft that his stablemaster was cruel and worthless, but it wasn't possible. He bit his tongue.

Part Seven

Chapter Seventeen

Two Years Later

"What are you still standing about here for, boy?" Silas thundered.

Jack flinched. Although he was now head and shoulders taller than the lame stablemaster, the words still landed like a lash on his back. Silas loomed in the stable door, leaning on his cane.

"The young master wants his horse brought around. Are you deaf, stupid, or both?" Silas snarled. "Shall I refresh your memory?"

It was no use telling Silas that Jack would fetch Warrior out in two minutes when he had finished skipping out Blackbird's stall. He merely ducked his head and said, "I'll do that, sir."

Silas scoffed. "You most assuredly will, you stupid boy. Why the master puts up with you, I'll never know!"

Jack kept his head down as he hurried across to Warrior's stall and brought out his saddle and bridle. As he ran a soft brush over the horse's satin-smooth coat, he habitually bent and felt over the forelimb that had so nearly ended his life. It remained as smooth and cool as ever.

"That's one good thing, old boy," Jack murmured.

"Are you muttering about me?" Silas shrieked across the yard.

"No, sir!" Jack cried. "Not at all. I'm talking to the horse, that's all."

Silas sneered. "You're a strange one as well as stupid, boy."

Jack knew that, after three years of this, he should be used to Silas' insults. Yet somehow their barbs always managed to sink below his skin.

To his relief, Silas shuffled off to rub liniment into his ever-worsening hip, and Jack was able to lose himself in the majesty of the big chestnut hunter. He worked the brush easily over the copper coat, oiled the hooves, laid the mane down with water, and then gently saddled him.

Warrior knew every motion he made; he stirred left and right as Jack moved around him in the box, and lifted his feet for the hoof pick with the steady familiarity of old friendship.

Jack smiled as he smoothed down the forelock and ran a soft rag over the horse's mouth and nose. "You're always here, old fellow," he murmured. "Aren't you?"

Warrior ran his lips over Jack's hand, wrinkling the silken skin in the way that always delighted him.

"Come on," said Jack. "There's a good chap."

He led the horse out at a smart clip, striding neatly beside him as they moved to the front of the house, where the young master already waited at the top of the steps. Impatiently tapping his riding crop against his boot. Warrior rolled his eyes at the sound. Mr. Ashcroft stood beside him, looking paler and more lined than even a week ago. He never rode out with the young master anymore; if the maids were to be believed, he did little other than work and drink these days.

"Don't ride too hard now," he was saying. "You still need to grow fit for the autumn hunting season."

"Oh, Father," said the young master, "as if you care. All you can think of is our summer visit to Annabel. You'll mope all year until we return there."

Mr. Ashcroft didn't correct his son's ridiculous manner.

The young master sneered with unabated hatred as Jack halted Warrior at the base of the steps.

"Another thing, Father," he sniped, "look at this old horse you've left me. Can't you see he's well past his prime?"

Jack's heart contracted. He looked up at Warrior, but to his eyes, the fine sprinkling of grey hairs around his eyes and down his nose only made the horse seem nobler and more heroic than ever.

"He is getting on, I suppose," said Mr. Ashcroft. He sighed. "I'm tired, son. I'll think of something later. Do go out and enjoy some fresh air..."

The master turned and trailed off into the house, and his son stomped down the steps in fi temper. He snatched the reins and vaulted onto his undeserving horse, then turned Warrior directly over Jack. Jack stumbled back, trying not to be trodden on, and the young master narrowly missed his face with the whip as he applied it to Warrior's shoulder and rode away at his usual careless gallop.

Jack stood and watched them go, wondering if Warrior would soon be gone too. If everything he cared about would slip away, just like Mama, Beryl, Reverend Samuel, Liz, and Finn.

The thought made his heart feel as heavy as a cannonball. He hung his head and trudged back to the stables, his chest weighed down with sorrow.

Jack's heart felt no lighter that evening as he topped up water buckets for the last time. In the waning summer, a lonely cricket chirped. The stable lantern lit his way as he moved from stable to stable, checking on each occupant. Cheerful lights glowed in Silas's cottage window; the loft was already dark and silent by comparison.

He set the bucket aside with his aching arms and plodded to the cottage for his ever-plundered ration. It waited on Silas' kitchen table, as usual; the old man had gone up to bed, leaving Jack to lock up and stoke his fire before retiring to the cold loft. But this time, none of it mattered. This time, a small white envelope lay beside Jack's plate on the table. He ignored the cold meat and cheese and snatched up the envelope at once.

Sure enough, her name was written on the back in her careful scrawl. *Beryl Nichols.*

Suddenly, Jack's heaviness evaporated. He was buoyed up, almost floating, as he strode to the loft with his plate in one hand and the letter in the other. As soon as he reached his bed of hay, he set the plate aside and carefully slit open the envelope, then withdrew the precious paper and carefully unfolded it before slowly savouring every word.

My dearest Jackie,

Autumn is much nicer here than it is in London. It's less rainy, and it smells better. We even have lots of sunny days. Annabel likes to sit by the window overlooking the beach then. I so wish you could see the beach, too. It's so lovely.

Jack closed his eyes and savoured the mental image of strolling along the beach with Beryl by his side, then read on.

Can you tell my writing is getting better? Annabel can seldom leave her room anymore, so we have done plenty of reading. Sometimes she grows too weary to read and I must do it for her, so I'm getting better at it.

It is sad but true that most of my walks on the beach are on my own now, and not as often as before. I don't like to leave Annabel's side. But we have fun, Jackie. We read and write, and we play games. I keep the fire very warm for her.

I hope you don't think I'm complaining, but I must tell you how very much I miss you every day. I so miss our afternoon conversations at lunchtime or our Sundays in the garden together, talking about everything. I miss your kind smile, your gentle voice, and your laugh. Our visit to London was so brief this summer... and yet you only seem to be kinder, gentler, and handsomer, with even better humour than before.

How are you, and how is Warrior?

I miss you, my Jackie. I hope we will be reunited soon. Every day, I pray to see you soon again.

With all my love,

Beryl.

Jack raised the letter to his lips and closed his eyes, inhaling the sweet puff of perfume she always left on her letters to him. It didn't smell like her—the perfume was too expensive for her to wear; Annabel insisted on lending it to her for her letters—but it smelled fresh and exciting and sweet, like Jack always felt when he saw her.

She was right. It had been so long.

He rummaged among his things for pencil and paper and, huddled by the small lantern, composed his response. He'd send it right away; he'd been saving for the postage all week.

My sweet Beryl,

First, let me tell you that Patty from the kitchen sends her regards. She always loved bringing up meals to you and Annabel and asks after you every time. Reverend Samuel and Mrs. Brownstone also send their love. I think Warrior does too, though it's hard to tell!

He is getting on in years but as spry as ever. I hope that the master will continue to keep him. The young master is getting tired of him, like he's an old toy.

Silas is as cruel as ever, but I try to be gentle and good. He often doesn't make it easy. The work only grows as he gets older and more lame, and he gets more and more cruel when the weather gets cold and his leg hurts more. I know it must be difficult but he does make work so wearisome at times.

How I wish I could walk on the beach with you! I long to see you again. I miss you, my sweet Beryl, every part of you—from your voice to the way you move your hands when you speak. I hope that one day everything will be right again, my love. That someday, our dreams will come true, and we can finally be together.

I miss you with all my heart.

Love, Jack.

My Jackie.

The words came back to Jack over and over as he worked, making him smile as he worked saddle soap over the fine leather of the harness. Beryl's letter had come only two days ago and already Jack had memorized every word like a passionate student with a classic poem. But it was those two words he kept coming back to, the words *my Jackie*, the ones that told him that he belonged to someone who found him wonderful and precious.

"What are you smiling about?" Silas barked, stumbling past with the bits he'd washed. "I'll wipe that grin clean off your face if you haven't finished those harnesses by lunch, you stupid boy!"

Jack's smile faded of its own accord. "Yes, sir," he mumbled demurely.

He gently wiped a clump of dried sweat from the leather's stitching and held back a deep sigh.

Across the yard, Warrior tossed his head and snorted.

A moment later, Jack, too, heard the clattering of hooves, and a pretty little black pony trotted into the yard drawing a comfortable light trap. Jack instantly recognized it. It had stopped at Ashcroft Manor many a time before Annabel left for the country; the black pony was a familiar guest in their stables. It spotted Jack and let out a friendly nicker, perhaps hoping for its usual rub-down and sweet mash.

All the same, worry tightened in Jack's belly. Why hadn't the coachman driven around to the front as he was meant to? Why come to the stables?

Who was so deathly ill that he could not spare a moment to wait?

Silas hurried from the tack room, pale at the impropriety. "Sir!" he cried. "I'm so very sorry. If this stupid boy would keep his ears open, we would know when we were wanted at the house." He shot Jack a venomous glare.

Dr. Whitmore disembarked from his carriage, barely looking at Silas. "Not to worry, my good man. I'm here for a reason. I would very much like to talk to Jack, please."

"Jack?" Silas gaped, shocked that Dr. Whitmore knew Jack's name. "The stable lad?"

"Yes, please. That would be most kind," said Dr. Whitmore.

Jack slowly lowered the harness onto a rail and shuffled a little nearer. Silas glared at him, but before he could say anything, Dr. Whitmore spotted him.

"Ah, Jack, there you are," he said. "Could you spare a moment of your time?"

"Yes, sir." Jack edged closer. "How may I help, sir?"

Dr. Whitmore smiled. "There's no need to look so nervous, my boy. In fact, you might be very pleased with the news I'm here to give you."

"I might?" Jack managed.

"Indeed." Dr. Whitmore laughed. "You see, my excellent stablemaster is getting on in years. He has decided it is time to spend the rest of his days at leisure in the country. He is a good man and deserves every moment of his happiness, but you understand that that leaves me without someone capable to care for my horses."

Wild hope frolicked in Jack's heart. "I... I understand, sir."

"I think you do," said Dr. Whitmore, "though you're not giving yourself permission to believe it yet." He smiled. "You see, Jack, ever since the night when you rode to my house on that fine-spirited hunter in that dreadful storm, I've known that you share a special touch with horses. I happen to be good friends with dear Samuel, too, and he gave me the most glowing recommendation."

Jack nodded. Samuel often spoke of his childhood friendship with Dr. Whitmore.

"All that, dear boy, is to tell you that I'm here to offer you work," said the doctor. "I would like you to come to my house and act as my stablemaster. There is a comfortable cottage over the stables that you would call your own, and I think you would find the compensation most competitive."

Jack's jaw dropped. He knew it was rude, but couldn't help gaping at the doctor open-mouthed, barely processing the words that the esteemed gentleman spoke. It was Silas who overcame his astonishment first.

"Dr. Whitmore!" he burst out. "You're making a terrible mistake, sir."

Dr. Whitmore raised an eyebrow. "And why is that, pray tell?"

"You've never seen a lazier boy in your life," Silas burst out. "He's a real layabout. He'll never be able to work unsupervised; I have to chase after him with a whip half the day as it is. Nor does he have any knowledge of horses. He'll have your whole stables colicking within the week."

Dr. Whitmore frowned. "As far as Mr. Ashcroft tells it, young Jack here is single-handedly responsible for the recovery of his son's prize hunter from a ligament injury. I know that not every horseman is capable of such."

Silas' face turned purple with rage. "Only because of my guidance, sir. Only because I forced him to do his work!"

Dr. Whitmore turned to Jack. "Is this true, Jack?"

Jack looked into Silas' eyes. He wouldn't lie to Dr. Whitmore, and he didn't look away as he spoke his quiet victory. "No, sir, it is not."

"I believe you," said Dr. Whitmore.

"Sir!" Silas burst out.

"Mr. Thorne," said Dr. Whitmore, "I believe that this conversation does not concern you."

Silas' lip twisted. He turned and stomped away.

Dr. Whitmore smiled as he turned to Jack. "So, how about it, young man? Would you like to come and work for me?"

Jack cast a single glance at Warrior's box, but already, a plan was forming in his mind. A plan that might actually be possible with the work Dr. Whitmore had offered him. "Yes, sir," he said.

"I would like that very much."

"Very well. I will discuss the matter with Mr. Ashcroft for you," said the doctor.

As the doctor's carriage pulled away, Jack stood still for a moment, a sense of hope and determination filling his chest. He took a deep breath, feeling for the first time in a long while that things might just start to change.

.

Chapter Eighteen

Jack sat at his writing desk in the little sitting room at the back of the cottage. A cup of hot tea—with milk and sugar—steamed at his elbow as the new pen moved smoothly across the nice, white paper.

Now I must go and start morning exercise, my love, but I hope to hear from you very soon. I've enclosed money for stamps, paper, and ink, so that you can write back whenever you please.

He gazed out of the window at the little garden behind his cottage, which lay still and dormant in the crisp fall morning but for a birdbath where a red-breasted robin doused himself in the shower of bright droplets.

One more thing, my dear, he added, *I want you to know that I will see you very, very soon. I do not yet have the full details of my plan, but it is a good one. Lord willing, you may hear my knock at your door far sooner than you may expect.*

Reverend Samuel, Mrs. Brownstone, and Dr. Whitmore send their regards. Please give my greetings to Annabel.

With all my love,

Jack.

He folded the nice paper carefully, making the creases neat and sharp, and then tucked it into his coat before he finished his tea and strolled through the cosy little kitchen and into the beautiful stable yard. The row of loose boxes was whitewashed, with bright blue doorframes and window shutters and hanging planters holding late marigolds and petunias in cheery colours.

Jack whistled. Even after only a few short months, a cacophony of nickers and whinnies came in response. Half a dozen noble heads looked out over the box doors. There was the splendid team of greys who drew Dr. Whitmore's flashy four-in-hand carriage, and the pretty black pony who pulled the trap, and a handsome raw-boned hack that took him for a leisurely turn around the park every Saturday morning.

Jack loved them all, and it was evident in their tidy manes, shining coats, and bright, soft eyes.

"They sure know your voice, Mr. Jack," said a thatch-haired boy a few years Jack's junior as he emerged from the tack room, carrying a bridle and saddle.

Jack chuckled. "They're intelligent creatures, Donnie." He stroked the black pony's nose. "Aren't they magnificent?"

"Always," said Donnie, starry-eyed. He carried the saddle and bridle into the hack's box.

Jack leaned on the door. "You say that old Twilight ate all her breakfast this morning?"

"Licked the platter clean, too, sir. You were right. A few minutes' grazing did her the world of good," said Donnie.

"Excellent. Do the same for her this afternoon, and you can give her corn again in the morning," said Jack. "You'll remember to clean Firework's tack when he comes back from his exercise, won't you?"

"Yes, sir," said Donnie.

A bell clanged suddenly by the stable wall, its cable disappearing into the towering brick wall of Dr. Whitmore's house. Jack and Donnie instantly abandoned all else and sprang into action. They threw the harness on the four-in-hand in a matter of minutes, and Jack led out two of them to harness to the ever-waiting carriage in the corner. By the time he had hitched them to the carriage, Donnie stood ready with the other two.

"Thank you, Donnie." Jack buckled the last piece of harness, then vaulted onto the carriage. "Up, boys! Get up!"

The four-in-hand clattered from the yard, their hooves flying high, their nostrils blowing wide. Gripping multiple sets of reins, Jack steered them to the front of the house just as Dr. Whitmore hurried downstairs, black bag in hand, tucking his bowler hat onto his head.

"Where to, sir?" Jack cried.

"Laurel Road, Jack, with all speed." Dr. Whitmore sprang into the carriage. "Young Master Batewell's had an accident."

"Yes, sir," said Jack.

He snapped the whip in the air and sang out, "Up, boys! Up!" and the four-in-hand flew down the drive, their combined strength making the carriage speed along. Jack felt the wind on his face and couldn't help smiling despite their urgent errand.

The horses' gleaming muscles churned ahead of him, their manes flew, their hooves clattered, and Jack knew that he was doing his part to help others.

All the same, a pang ran through him as he turned the horses onto the road and let them fly at their best pace. Beryl always talked about how much she loved to see Dr. Whitmore's four-in-hand when he arrived at Ashcroft Manor to see Annabel. She would have adored riding on the carriage beside him, or even simply petting the horses and feeding them carrots.

And then there was Mama...

Jack felt tears sting his eyes. He wondered if his desperate mother had ever had the privilege of riding on a carriage, let alone driving a magnificent four-in-hand like this. He wondered if she would have been proud to see him driving the doctor's carriage like this. He longed to find out. He closed his eyes for a moment, holding onto the hope that he might find out someday.

Jack carried a saddle over one arm and a bridle over his shoulder, and despite the harsh nip of winter in the air, he was sweating as he laboured up the long path to the stables at Ashcroft Manor.

It had been three months since he'd walked away from this place and promised himself that he'd never return. And yet here he was, tired and sweaty, his feet aching from the long walk, striding up the same pathway he'd always taken from too-brief visits to St. Luke's when he returned to his cold sleeping space in the loft. The manor house looked quieter and more grim than ever as it loomed over the snow-dusted lawns. Silas' angry yells echoed from the stable yard, and each one lashed over Jack's shoulders.

He cleared his throat, taking courage, and marched into the stable yard in the nick of time. Silas was already leading Warrior out into the yard. Jack's heart broke at the sight of the fine animal. He'd lost weight since Jack had left, and his once penny-bright coat was dull. But when he spotted Jack, he threw up his head and emitted a trumpeting neigh.

Silas yanked on the plain white halter. "Shut up, you beast!"

Warrior flung his head. The old stablemaster had no hope of holding onto him; the rope tore through his fingers, and Warrior galloped across the yard to Jack with his tail flagging. Jack seized the rope and the horse halted without pulling, then butted his silken nose into Jack's face.

Silas' face twisted into that familiar, thunderous sneer. "You," he snarled.

Jack stared at him. Somehow, the monstrous being who had tormented his years was gone. In his place stood a sad, crippled old man who took out his jealousy, chronic pain, and miscellaneous vices on an innocent and harmless boy. Jack had expected to feel fear or even anger when he came back here. Instead, he throbbed with something very different: pity.

"Come crawling back to your good work here, did you?" Silas sneered. "Realized that you didn't have it so hard after all, you ungrateful lout?"

"Not exactly, Mr. Thorne," said Jack.

Silas blinked, as though taking in for the first time the fact that Jack wore a warm coat and jodhpurs.

"Were you on your way to the sale with Warrior?" Jack enquired.

"That's right," Silas snapped. "Old horse is too slow for the young master now. Give him back." He extended a hand.

Jack laid the saddle on the ground at his feet and rooted in his pocket for a clinking coin pouch. He remembered dreaming of having pounds one day when he was a boy.

This was his first time owning any more money than a single pound; he had saved every penny except for what he bought in food and tiny luxuries, like a new pen for writing to Beryl, or a warm coat to replace the threadbare one he'd had before.

Or jodhpurs to make riding easier. Riding would soon be an even more important part of his life.

"There's no need, Mr. Thorne," said Jack. "You won't have to take Warrior to the sale anymore." He held out the pouch.

Silas scoffed. "I've been told to get the best price possible for this animal, boy." He overturned the pouch over his hand. "Not the kind of pittance that—" He stopped short, eyes widening.

"I think you'll find that's significantly more than the average old hunter will fetch at a sale," said Jack. "In fact, I believe Mr. Ashcroft will be more than satisfied with you if you bring him that."

Silas shut his mouth with a snap. Jack was right, and the cruel old man couldn't deny it.

"Do we have a deal?" Jack prompted.

Silas gazed at the money, then sneered again. "It'll do."

"Thank you kindly." Jack swung his saddle onto Warrior's back, then swiftly replaced the rough halter with a newly oiled bridle. With an effortless spring, he was back on Warrior, reins gathered in his hand, chin high. Warrior pawed the ground in excitement. Jack laughed at the familiar power underneath him.

"Go, old boy!" he said. "Go!"

Warrior snorted and bounded forward with the boldness of a horse half his age. They cantered down Ashcroft Manor's driveway for the last time, Jack's whoops and laughs combining with Warrior's snorts. When they reached the road, Jack did not turn back for Dr. Whitmore's house. Instead, he aimed Warrior's head for the open road, and for the country.

The Ashcroft's' country house was a far less imposing affair than the manor in London. As they rode over the hill and Jack's gaze alighted on the address to which he'd asked directions from Dr. Whitmore, his heart leaped. This was, indeed, a beautiful place for sweet Beryl to have spent the past year.

Though splendid still, the house had curving gables and large, arched windows, and it was half the size of the manor. Even so, it took Jack some time to walk the hot, sweaty Warrior around its outside, passing lawns and rose gardens before they reached the vegetable patch and the small stables. Only one little pony whinnied at Warrior from the boxes there. Jack walked the last half-mile, and when they reached the tie ring over the water trough in the stable yard, he had only to tie Warrior and pat his neck before he strode up to the servants' entrance.

He glanced at his reflection in a nearby window and straightened his cap and tie before he knocked. A rosy-cheeked cook opened the door.

"Yes?" she said.

"Excuse me, ma'am," said Jack, "do you know if Beryl is in?"

"Dear Beryl's always in, my boy. She's got little choice with Annabel to look after and all." The cook's eyes narrowed. "Who are you?"

"Could you tell her that Jack Finch is here to see her?" Jack asked.

"Jack Finch!" The cook's eyes widened. "In the flesh!"

"Ah, I suppose so," said Jack.

The cook laughed. "Beryl talks so much about you, I thought you were a ghost. Come in, dear boy, come in."

The cook ushered him into a cosy kitchen that smelled of onions and boiling broth, and a housemaid was sent scurrying off while the cook plied him with tea. It was only a few moments later, but felt like an eternity, when Beryl appeared like an angelic vision in the doorway.

Jack almost dropped his teacup. If possible, she had only grown more beautiful in the months since he'd last seen her. Her hair was neatly pulled back, a rich bright fringe around her pale face, and her eyes shone like fragments of the sky.

"Beryl," Jack croaked.

Her eyes filled with tears. "Oh, Jackie!"

She sped across the kitchen to him, and he grasped her hands and longed to shower her with kisses. But that would all come in good time. She was almost crying as she gazed into his eyes, and in the tightness around her mouth, he read the true story of Annabel's health and the many hours she spent nursing her charge.

"How?" Beryl cried, half-laughing. "How did you get here? Did you take the stagecoach?"

"I did not, my dear." Jack beamed. "The only reason I haven't done so yet is because I've been saving for something far better." He gripped her arm. "Come with me."

Beryl giggled in anticipation as he led her outside to where splendid Warrior stood tied to the wall, water droplets sparkling on his whiskers, his coat vibrant in the sun.

"Warrior!" Beryl cried, wide-eyed. "But—but what is he doing here?"

"The stagecoach is fast," Jack acknowledged, "but a good horse is even faster. My position at Dr. Whitmore's includes room and board and one stable." He smiled. "I can visit you every Sunday afternoon now, my love, and still be home in time for evening stables."

Tears welled in Beryl's eyes. "Every Sunday afternoon," she breathed.

"Every week," Jack promised.

Beryl clasped her hands to her face, overcome with joy, and Jack's heart welled within him. She didn't know that this was only the beginning of the many joys he had planned for her.

"It won't be long anymore, my love," he said quietly.

"What do you mean?" Beryl raised her head.

Jack hesitated. He knew that he would next be saving for an engagement ring and all that was needed to marry this beautiful girl, this soulmate.

But there was one great dilemma, even greater than money, that stood in his way: Annabel. He couldn't ask Beryl to leave her.

"You'll find out," he said finally, squeezing her hand, and she forgot her confusion in the rapture of the moment. If only Jack could do the same.

Winter passed in an ecstasy of cold mornings spent exercising the horses, afternoons of adjusting rugs and adding extra straw to stables, and Sundays that were a blur of joy on Warrior's back.

Journeys that had seemed impossible on foot were nothing to the bold horse's four strong legs. Jack rode to St. Luke's every Sunday morning for church and sat under Reverend Samuel's teaching, then shared a cup of tea with Mrs. Brownstone before he undertook the journey to the country village where Beryl lived.

They spent many quiet evenings in the kitchen, talking quietly as the cook chaperoned.

When the days grew longer, their visits moved outside as springtime brought a green flush to the hills and turned the ocean to azure instead of winter's bitter grey-green. As mistress of the house, Annabel was the one whose permission meant anything, and in her parents' absence she allowed Jack and Beryl to stroll through the rose garden as if they were wealthy folk.

The rose garden smelled of pure sweetness, yet not as sweet as Beryl's hair. She walked slowly beside Jack, her hand on his arm, her precious warmth so near him. The sunshine warmed the top of her bonnet and her dress's hem hissed gently on the cool, deep grass that crunched under their feet with moisture.

"Look at this one," said Beryl, pausing to touch a bright yellow rose. "Isn't it lovely? I think I'll have the gardener cut a bunch for Annabel's room. They'll brighten the place."

"That's a lovely idea." Jack squeezed her hand. "How is Annabel today? I noticed she didn't come down to say hello. Not that I expect her to—it's most kind of her to take notice of a lout like me." He laughed.

Beryl smiled. "Annabel's not like the others, you know. She doesn't consider anyone beneath her just because they're poorer or low-born."

"I know that," said Jack. "That's why you and she are such good friends."

Beryl's smile faded. "She wanted to greet you, Jack, but the truth is..." She shook her head. "Annabel hasn't been able to get out of bed for the past few days. In fact, I've persuaded her to write to Dr. Whitmore. I think he should see her."

"Is she ill?" Jack asked.

"Not in the usual way. There's no fever, no coughing. She just seems terribly weak." Beryl's lower lip trembled. "Jack, I... I think she's not long for this world."

Jack rubbed her hand. "Perhaps there's something Dr. Whitmore can do."

Beryl brushed at her tears. "I don't know. Perhaps. You'll pray for her, won't you?"

"Always," Jack promised.

Beryl swallowed and tried to smile. "I'm sorry. I don't mean to make our visits an unhappy occasion."

"Nothing could be unhappy with you by my side, my dear," said Jack.

They strolled on, and Jack fished for a lighter topic of conversation.

"Did I ever tell you that yellow is my mother's favourite colour?" he asked.

Beryl smiled. "You didn't. I love to hear about your mother. Have you had any luck finding her?"

Jack shook his head. "None, I'm afraid. I've been asking around for Mabel Finch, but no one seems to have heard of her. Reverend Samuel suggested putting an advertisement in the paper. I may save up for that next."

"An excellent idea," said Beryl. "I'd love to meet her someday."

"You know," said Jack, "it's been more than fourteen years since I lost her, but I still feel as though I know her. As though she's close to me somehow." He smiled. "I know that she'd love you."

Beryl leaned her head against his shoulder. "I do hope so."

They walked on through the spring garden, wrapped in the ardour of young love. There were many things Jack still longed to do. Marry Beryl, firstly—but secondly, to find his mother. Yet for now, the moment was as perfect as any moment could be.

Chapter Nineteen

Percy snapped the whip in the air above the carriage horse's toiling haunches. "Get on, girl," he called. "We're nearly there."

The horse put her head down and the light brougham rattled to the top of the hill, and the sea spread out before them, a magnificent carpet of glittering blue beneath the bright spring sunshine.

The pretty village lay along the beach, a lovely collection of cottages, farms, and a few wealthy homes popular among the London rich to escape to the seaside for a few days since it was less than two hours by horseback from North London.

It was also only forty minutes' drive from the Mitchell farm and had no lawyer, and so Percy frequently found himself taking this same road over the hill to the village, albeit not often on a Sunday afternoon as he did now.

The witness he had to prepare would be in court early the next morning, and he feared that the cowardly young man might not go to London unless Percy took him there himself. He would sleep over in an inn tonight, be ready to take his witness to London and spend the day in court tomorrow and the day after, and have time to stop by Nathan Goulding's office before he returned to dear Mabel and the children. They usually travelled with him, but poor Eddie had a bout of the flu and Mabel had to stay home to care for him.

The thought of being separated from his wife and children for two whole nights filled Percy with painful longing. How quiet the inn would seem without little feet pattering on the floors! How strangely empty the bed!

He could barely face the prospect of being without his children for two nights. It made his heart sting all the more for Mabel, who had now been searching for her Jack for almost fifteen years. Jack would no longer be a boy now, but a young man of eighteen or nineteen, strapping and strong.

If Jack still lived.

Percy slowed the horse to a walk and allowed her to meander down the hill as the afternoon shadows grew long on the fields. Poor, sweet Mabel.

He had given her more children and a life that he knew she loved, yet he knew that none of it could soothe the loss of Jack and the pain of not knowing what had become of him. Nathan had still made no headway in searching for Jack, though Percy knew that the investigator was doing his best.

The clatter of hooves made his horse lift her head. Percy looked up, too, surprised that he would meet someone else on this deserted stretch of road. A beautiful chestnut hunter with a copper-shiny coat and white stripe on his face came cantering along the road toward them. His rider politely reined him down to a bolt trot as they neared the carriage and doffed his cap. He was a young man, not yet twenty, with a lovely, smiling face and freckles that seemed familiar somehow. Percy couldn't help returning the smile.

The chestnut hunter rode away, and Percy felt a sudden burst of vigour. It was as if the young man's energy and brightness had given him hope somehow. He snapped the whip, pushing the horse into a brisk trot. Perhaps he'd go around the village this evening and ask if anyone he saw knew somebody called Jack Finch.

It was a long shot, but Percy was willing to try. He'd try anything to bring Mabel's little boy back.

Wild knocking jerked Jack from his comfortable slumber. He raised his head with a gasp as more knocking resounded on his cottage door, and panic clutched him. An emergency for Dr. Whitmore, and the bell perhaps broken? Or a colicking horse that lay cast in its stall, hooves against the wall, guts hopelessly knotted? The latter terrified him. He hated few things more than seeing one of his charges in pain.

Jack scrambled out of bed, threw on his coat, and ran to the door. He turned up the gas lamp and flung the door wide open. "What is it?" he cried. "What's wrong?"

It was the butler. His face was drawn and pale from sleep, and the usually spotless man seemed odd in his nightclothes.

"Dr. Whitmore has called for you at once," he said.

Jack shook the last sleep from his head. "I'll harness the carriage."

"No, no," said the butler, "not yet. He must speak with you first."

"Why?" Jack asked.

"I don't know, boy," said the butler, "but you had better hurry; he seemed most put out."

Confused, Jack pulled on his boots over bare toes and sprinted through the spring chill to the servants' entrance. A sleepy-eyed chambermaid directed him upstairs to a part of the grand house that Jack had never dreamed to see. He barely glimpsed the beautiful paintings and expensive velvet drapes; all he saw was Dr. Whitmore sitting in a paisley chair, his hand to his mouth, the other clutching a note.

"Dr. Whitmore, sir, are you all right?" Jack cried, startled by the beloved old man's pale complexion.

Dr. Whitmore raised his head. "Dear boy, I'm afraid my heart is broken, and so will yours be." He paused. "Annabel has gone to her Saviour's arms."

Jack stumbled to a halt, his heart freezing. First, it stung for poor Annabel, who had always been so unusually kind. Then, it broke for Beryl. "She—she's passed on, sir?"

"I'm afraid so," said Dr. Whitmore. "The note just came from Beryl. She died quietly in her sleep. But poor Beryl! She'll be heartbroken. I called you because I believe she needs you, dear boy."

Jack hesitated. "Sir, the horses."

"Donnie will be all right for a day. Go to her," said Dr. Whitmore. "For all the respect I have for Mr. Ashcroft, I fear that Beryl might find herself with nowhere to go unless you give her somewhere. She should not be alone, Jack. You may have the day tomorrow to do whatever you need."

Overcome with Dr. Whitmore's kindness, Jack felt his throat close with tears. "Sir, I don't know how to thank you."

Dr. Whitmore gazed at the note for a moment, then up at Jack. "I was a very little boy when I had scarlet fever," he said. "I should not have lived, but a doctor fought for my life and saved me. Ever since, though my wealth made it unnecessary, all I wanted was to heal others as he healed me. If I can do that in medicine, so be it. But if there are other ways to do so, then I will use those, too. Go to Beryl, Jack, and may the Lord's angels ride with you."

Afterward, Jack remembered little about that ride through the darkness except that Warrior never put a foot wrong, and that the miles slipped past beneath his flying hooves in what seemed like minutes, and that the dawn was breaking pale grey over the sea when he galloped over the horizon and saw the village spread out beneath them like a bowl of lights on the edge of the sea's abyss.

He ran the last half-mile beside his horse and jogged into the stable yard calling, "Beryl! Beryl, my love! I'm here!"

He'd barely stripped Warrior of his saddle when the back door crashed open and Beryl flew into his arms. Grief had stripped her of inhibition. She wrapped her arms around him and buried her face in his chest, and Jack could not but put his arms around her slender body and stroke her untamed tumult of scarlet hair as she wept and wept into his chest.

It was a long time before her crying abated and she finally raised her head from Jack's chest.

"Oh, Jackie," she croaked, "I'm so tired. I'm so very tired."

Jack brushed her tear-streaked hair from her face. "I know." He paused. "My heart hurts for you, my dear, but you should know that sweet Annabel is safe now, free from pain. If there are beaches in Heaven, she's not only strong enough to walk on them now, but to run."

The smile that lifted Beryl's face collided with the tears in her eyes, but it was full and genuine. "She's free now," she said. "The last thing she told me before she died was that she couldn't wait to taste the fruits of Heaven."

"Now she's tasting them, my love," Jack soothed.

Beryl shivered, as if only now noticing the chill in the air. Jack put an arm around her shoulders; the groom had come to take Warrior, and Jack led her into the kitchen.

"I don't know what will happen now, Jack," Beryl whispered. "I'm... I'm scared."

Jack steered her into a stool, then crouched beside her and laid a hand on her knee. "There's no need to be afraid," he said. "Everything will be all right. Dr. Whitmore tells me that there are good rooms to rent in an inn not far from his house. I will take you back to London when you've had a little sleep, and you'll stay in the rooms."

"I haven't any money," Beryl quavered. "The Ashcrofts never paid me except in board, lodge, and clothes. Annabel gave me money when I needed anything else."

"You don't need money. I'll pay for it," said Jack. "Don't worry about such things now. Dr. Whitmore wishes to go to Annabel's funeral, too, so you won't miss it."

Beryl exhaled, her shoulders shaking. "Oh, Jack," she whispered, "thank the Lord for you. What would I ever do without you?"

Jack met her eyes.

"You never have to do without me," he said.

It seemed to Jack at times that nowhere in the world could be as beautiful as Hyde Park at the height of summer. The beautifully trimmed hedges and shrubbery, the deep expanses of dark green lawns that were so rich and springy beneath one's feet, and the mirror-smooth ponds on which the trees so magnificently painted their reflections all spoke to him of utter peace and serenity.

He walked slowly, Beryl's hand wrapped in his, a picnic basket over his arm. The tiny but wonderful weight of the small object in his pocket reminded him of its presence with every step.

"When we were little children working for Smudge, would you have believed anyone who told us that a place like this existed in London?" he asked.

Beryl tipped her head back to smile at him from beneath the fringe of the new lace parasol he'd bought for her as a gift. "Not at all," she said. "I thought that all London was like the parts we saw; ugly, dirty, and smelly, with hungry children and frightening chimney sweeps everywhere."

"Those children are still out there," Jack murmured. "It's only by the grace of God that we escaped."

"He has orchestrated it all," said Beryl. "Now look at us." She laughed. "Two urchins who once swept chimneys, walking in Hyde Park on a Sunday afternoon. Isn't it wonderful?"

"It's more than wonderful," said Jack. "I think it's almost perfect."

Her lip quirked upward. "Only almost?"

He chuckled. "All right, it's perfect."

They reached a shady spot between three trees who spread their branches over the deep grass. Beryl stood to one side, holding the basket, as Jack spread a tartan rug on the ground. She perched delicately on the blanket, her legs demurely folded, and opened the basket, from which she unpacked the cold repast she'd assembled: ham and cheese, apples, and thick slices of buttered bread, with pickled onions on the side and a bounty of lemon cordial.

"A perfect summer picnic," said Jack, sitting cross-legged across from her.

Beryl laughed. "There's that word again."

As they increasingly had done over the past few months while Beryl lived at the inn, they ate in silence. Their conversation was as lovely as ever, yet there were times now when the companionable quiet that settled between them seemed more powerful and more loving than any amount of chatter ever could. It was utterly comfortable and at ease, the silence of two people who no longer had anything to prove to one another, and Jack revelled in it.

Today, though, as the ham, cheese, and apples disappeared, nervousness rose in his belly. He forced himself not to show it, talking and laughing with Beryl as though all was well with the world. And all *was* well, truth be told. Better than well—perfect and wonderful. The nervousness held no fear, merely the quivering tension of knowing that he was approaching one of the most important moments of his existence.

At last only a heel of bread was left, the way it always was after one of their picnics.

"Look at this!" said Beryl, picking it up as they cleared away the paper wrappings. "The duckies will love this."

She always said it, yet it never failed to make Jack smile at the fond inflection on *duckies*.

"I'll fold the rug," he said. "You feed the ducks. I'll be with you in a moment."

Unwitting, she strode away to break the bread into pieces and throw it on the surface of the nearest pond, where it drifted like snowflakes before the brightly coloured mallards paddled over to eat. Her laugh at their dabbling was melodic, lifting Jack's heart, giving him the kick of courage he needed for what came next.

He reached into his pocket for the ring—a slender silver band, nothing fancy, yet it represented many hours of hard labour. At the same time, those hours felt inadequate to express how he felt about the girl standing on the pond's bank, rising onto her tiptoes as she cast fistfuls of bread to the ducks, her scarlet hair catching the dappled light, her laughter catching his soul.

Jack approached her slowly, drawing the ring from his pocket, and sank to one knee. He tried to say, "Beryl," in a deep and warm and manly voice; the only thing that came out was a strangled little squeak.

She turned, and the concern in her jewel-bright eyes dissolved gloriously into shocked joy.

Those eyes shone, more brilliant than the brightest spring sky, and she raised her trembling hands to her lips as they curved into an incredulous, overjoyed smile.

"J-Jack," she croaked. "Oh, Jackie!"

Jack had to clear his throat twice before he could speak. "My dream has always been you," he whispered. "You forgave me. You loved me constantly, even when I left you. You never wavered. For the rest of your life, I want to return that love. I want to be steadfast for you, a lighthouse in the storm. I want to be—"

"Oh, Jackie," she croaked, "please, just ask me! I can't wait another moment!"

Jack laughed, tears of joy stinging his eyes. "Beryl Nichols, will you marry me?"

She cried the word "Yes!" almost before he could reach the end of the question. Her slender hands trembled as she extended them to him. Jack rose, his hands shaking so much with excitement that he was barely able to slide the ring onto her delicate digit.

No sooner had he slipped the ring onto her finger, making her his fiancée, than she flew into his arms, holding him close and tight, as if trying to make up for all the years of separation, longing, and love in that one embrace. Jack hugged her back just as fiercely, his heart full to bursting. In her arms, he felt complete. Beryl reached up and wiped a small tear from the corner of his eye. "What is it, Jackie?"

He smiled softly, his emotions a mix of overwhelming joy and a quiet ache. "I'm so happy, Beryl. Happier than I've ever been. It's just... there's still a part of me that wishes my mother could be here, to see this, to see us."

Beryl nodded, understanding. "I know," she whispered. "But we'll find her, Jackie. I believe we will."

Jack took a deep breath, letting her words settle into his heart. Even in this moment of happiness, he knew a piece of him would always be searching. But with Beryl beside him, he felt ready to face whatever came next. Life wasn't perfect, but it was as close as he could hope for. And that was enough to fill him with hope for the future.

Part Eight

Epilogue –

One Year Later

Jack and Beryl

Summer's dusk settled over the Whitmore stables, casting long shadows that stretched like fingers across the stable yard. Jack moved quickly, his boots crunching on the gravel with a sense of urgency. Usually, he took his time here, pausing at each stall to speak softly to the horses, to stroke their muzzles or offer a treat. But tonight, his heart was racing, and he barely registered the familiar sights and sounds around him.

Warrior, his old favourite, whinnied from the end stall, expecting his usual carrot. "In a minute, old fellow!" Jack called out, his voice breathless with excitement. He couldn't stop now—not when the news he'd discovered was burning inside him like a fire.

He pushed open the door to his cottage, where warmth and the savoury smell of garlic and beef filled the air. The fire crackled in the hearth, casting a golden glow over the small, cosy room. Beryl stood at the table, her knife moving in a steady rhythm as she chopped vegetables for the stew simmering on the stove.

She looked up, laughing as Jack burst in, his hair tousled from the wind. "Jackie, my love! How many times must I remind you to wipe your feet when you come in from the yard?"

"There's no time for that!" Jack exclaimed, sweeping her into his arms. He spun her around, her laughter filling the room like a bright, joyful melody.

"Jack!" Beryl protested, her smile wide. "You'll cause an accident with that potato in one hand and a paring knife in the other."

He set her back on her feet, still holding her close, his heart pounding not just from his hurried run but from the words he was about to say. He kissed her, a quick, eager kiss, then pulled back just enough to see her face. "Beryl, you won't believe it. I finally have news."

She put the knife down, her eyes widening with anticipation. "News? What news, Jackie?"

"The workhouse," Jack said, his voice brimming with excitement. "I went there again today, just as I have so many times before, hoping for any scrap of information. And this time, I found something. Someone was willing to help."

Beryl's face softened, her hands reaching for his. "Is it about your mother?" she asked quietly, almost afraid to hope.

"It is," Jack replied, squeezing her fingers. "I spoke to an old porter there. He remembered the records—knew where they were kept. We found her name, Beryl. Mabel Finch. She was there, but not anymore."

Beryl's breath caught. "She left?"

Jack nodded, his voice steady despite his racing heart. "She hasn't been there for over fifteen years. She left not long after I did. And the porter remembered more. A young gentleman, kind and well-dressed, took her away. Someone who was good to her."

"Not your father?" Beryl asked, her brow furrowing.

"No, not him," Jack replied. "Mama always said he was gone, long gone. But whoever took her from that place, they were kind to her. That's what matters."

Beryl's eyes sparkled with a mixture of relief and anticipation. "Then she could be out there somewhere, looking for you."

Jack nodded, pulling her close, feeling the steady beat of her heart against his own. "The porter said someone came by, years ago, asking for me. A man. I don't know who, but he was looking for a Jack Finch."

"Do you think she sent him?" Beryl whispered.

"I hope so," Jack said, his voice thick with emotion. "I hope she's still out there, looking for me. Just as I've been looking for her."

Beryl wrapped her arms around him, holding him close. "We'll find her, Jackie. I know we will. And until then, we have each other."

Jack leaned in, his forehead resting against hers, feeling the warmth of her breath on his skin. "I love you, Beryl," he murmured.

"I love you always," she replied, her voice soft but firm, anchoring him to this moment, to the life they were building together.

They stood there, entwined in each other's arms, the firelight flickering around them. Jack's mind buzzed with the possibilities, the paths that lay ahead. But here, in this quiet moment with Beryl, he felt a sense of purpose. Whatever the future held, they would face it side by side.

And as the night deepened, Jack knew they would find their way, one step at a time, together.

Mabel and Percy

Mabel Mitchell stood at the edge of her field, a hand resting on her growing belly. The wind was cool, rustling the leaves of the nearby trees, carrying with it the rich scent of earth and new growth. The farm was quiet today, a soothing contrast to the noise and chaos of London she had left behind. She breathed in deeply, feeling the baby kick gently inside her, a small, reassuring presence amid the emptiness she felt without Jack.

Her body ached from the day's work, but the pain was a comfort—a reminder that she was still alive, still moving forward. But even in this peace, there was always a part of her that remained restless. Little Jack. Her thoughts never wandered far from him, the son she hadn't seen since he was taken from her in a London workhouse. She imagined him still there, navigating those same streets, his small face lost among the crowds. The thought brought a familiar ache to her chest.

She dug her fingers deeper into the earth, grounding herself in the work. It was what she did to keep herself from falling into despair. The physical effort was exhausting, but it was a welcome distraction from the worry that gnawed at her heart. She needed to feel the soil in her hands, the solid ground beneath her feet, to remind herself that she was here, that she had made it out.

"Mama, look!" Eddie's voice broke through her thoughts. She turned to see her son, beaming with pride, holding up a rock nearly the size of his head. He had carried it all the way across the field, a feat of strength for a boy his age.

"Well done, my boy," Mabel called back with a smile. "Come on, it's time to get ready for supper."

Maggie, her younger daughter, ran up with a bright ladybird perched on her finger. "Look, Mama! Isn't it pretty?"

"It's lovely, Maggie," Mabel said, laughing softly. She lifted her daughter onto Polly, their old chestnut mare. "Let's head back, shall we?"

The journey back to the farmhouse was filled with the sounds of Maggie's laughter and Eddie's proud recounting of his strength. Mabel listened, her heart full, yet always with a space held for Jack.

As they reached the yard, Percy stepped out, his warm smile greeting them. "Hello, my darlings!" he called. Maggie and Eddie ran to him, their voices mingling with joy.

Mabel watched her family, feeling the warmth spread through her. She knew the road ahead wouldn't be easy, and some parts of her past still lingered, unresolved. But she had found something precious here—love, safety, a chance to build a new life.

Inside, they gathered around the dinner table, the fire crackling softly. Mabel glanced toward the window, where a small lamp flickered—a beacon in the dark, a quiet hope for Jack's return. She placed her hand over Percy's, feeling his steady reassurance.

"We're doing okay, aren't we?" he said gently.

Mabel nodded. "Yes," she replied softly. "We're doing okay."

As the evening settled in around them, Mabel let herself find peace in the simple moments—the warmth of the fire, the laughter of her children, and the quiet strength that carried her forward. Tomorrow would bring its own challenges, but for tonight, surrounded by her family, she had everything she needed.

And that was enough.

Helen Nichols

Helen Nichols kept her head down as she hastened along the street. It was the only way to avoid the piercing stares of the men who shared the street with her, their eyes always looking straight through her, their leers never growing any less horrible. She could do nothing to stop them, so she avoided their gazes instead, keeping her eyes on the crowd straight ahead.

They were a silent, huddled, fast-moving lot, as hunched and hurried as she.

Like Helen, everyone on the street wore ragged clothes and smelled of smoke.

None looked up at the evening light that struck beams through the grey sky, hinting at something brighter and more lovely than the smog that perpetually hung over London's docks, as though a beautiful sunset lay just beyond the curtain of its industry's smoke and stench. Beauty was so scarce on these streets that the very idea of it had fled their minds.

Beauty was certainly far from Helen's mind. To her, summer meant nothing other than a slight easing of one aspect of survival. She could save a little money on coal and candles, perhaps. There still never seemed to be enough.

Helen's feet throbbed as she turned down a slightly broader street. Here, it was important to stay as invisible as possible. Those who walked here were far from wealthy, but their cheap clothes were often new, and they held the fierce pride of those who were one step above the breadline and considered themselves infinitely superior to those who were one step below.

In the fading light, Helen's vision often blurred. She had to squint to make sure she was walking toward the right store. She ducked down an alley, avoiding a gentleman who looked ready to cuff her on the ear, and slunk to the back door of the slop-shop on this bustling street.

She knocked twice, then stepped back. It was a good thing, too. The door crashed open with such violence that it might have knocked her to the ground if she hadn't.

"You," the man in the doorway hissed. "You're late."

He was ponderously obese, his buttons straining over his mighty paunch, his eyes baleful pinpricks among the puffiness of his cheeks. His sneer twisted lips dusted with dirty stubble, a forgotten whisker straying to several inches' length here and there.

"I'm sorry, sir. I finished everything you gave me," Helen added hopefully, as though that would make any difference.

The man snorted. "I should hope you did. What do you seamstresses do all day?"

Helen hung her head. She'd made three coats in the past week from scratch, spending every day huddled over a stub of candle in her reeking tenement, trying to ignore the sounds of fighting and crying and coughing from all around her as she made out tiny stitches in the fading light.

"Three coats, sir," she croaked. "As promised."

She held out the fabric with trembling hands. The man snatched the coats, plucking them heartlessly this way and that as though they represented less than her very survival. He surveyed every seam with a critical eye, then finally huffed, as if disappointed that he hadn't found anything to condemn.

"Very well," he growled. "I suppose you want your money."

He reached into his pocket. It was all that Helen could do not to snatch the coins from his hand. She closed her fingers over them as soon as they struck her palm, and with the brisk economy of the starving, she knew immediately that there was not enough money. When she opened her hand, she saw it. A shilling and sixpence instead of two.

"Sir," she protested, "wh-what's this?"

"I told you to bring me that coat by seven," said the man. "It's ten past."

A church bell tolled.

"Excuse me," said the man, "it's a quarter past."

Helen's heart swelled to fill her throat. "But sir... the candles," she whispered. "They grow all the more expensive."

"What difference does it make to me, woman? I pay rent for the fine lodgings you share with the other seamstresses. You'll want me to provide you with food next!" The man shook his head. "Do you want next week's fabric, or would you rather sleep on the streets tonight?"

The thought struck a bolt of ice into Helen's chest. She'd spent too many of her nights on the street already.

"No, sir. The fabric, please, sir," she croaked.

The man smiled as though revelling in her tears. "That's what I thought." He produced a roll of cloth from inside the slop-shop and thrust it into Helen's hands. "Four pairs of men's trousers. I trust you will be on time this week."

"Of course, sir," Helen whispered.

The man slammed the door in her face without so much as a goodbye, and Helen turned and shuffled painfully back in the direction of the tumbledown marketplace several blocks from her, struggling to calculate what she would have to go without. Candles? No, but that was the only way she could keep working. Food, then? She was so desperate for a square meal...

Wandering disconsolately through the grimiest of London's streets, Helen could find nothing to hope for, nothing to look forward to. The present was a jumble of weariness, hunger, and misery. The future was an abyss of unknown terrors. Instead, as they always did when she felt herself slipping away, Helen's thoughts fled to a happy place in the past. A place where she'd cradled the most beautiful little girl in her arms. A child with scarlet hair, charming freckles, and the most wonderful pale blue eyes. They were so bright and piercing—bright as jewels.

The memory made tears sting her eyes, but at the same time, a smile curved her lips. It had been so long, and yet even now, the mere thought of her daughter made her heart sing.

"I'll find you someday, Beryl," she whispered. "I know you're out there. I'll find you."

New strength flooded her. Helen raised her head, squared her shoulders, and marched into the foul hubbub of the city.

Coming Soon

The Lost Mother's Christmas Miracle

If you are not already a subscriber to my newsletter and would like to be notified when The Lost Mother's Christmas Miracle is available please join my newsletter.

You will also receive a subscriber only book.

Join Iris Coles Newsletter

The Widow's Hope Book 1 Victorian Romance Saga

Little Jack Book 2 Victorian Romance Saga

List of Books

The Widow's Hope

The Little One's Christmas Dream

The Waif's Lost Family

The Pickpocket Orphans

The Workhouse Girls Despair

The Forgotten Match Girl's Christmas Birthday

The Wretched Needle Worker

The Lost Daughter

The Christmas Pauper

Printed in Great Britain
by Amazon